Athena raised her hands toward Medusa and began chanting:

> *"Hair-proud goddess, vain and haughty,*
> *How you'll wish you'd never been naughty.*
> *How you'll weep for insulting Athena,*
> *Some goddesses are mean, but I'm much meaner!*
> *When you look in a mirror, you'll get shivers and*
> *   shakes,*
> *Your long thick hair is now a nest of snakes!"*

Instantly, Medusa's hair twisted itself into dozens of long, dark braids. The braids began to pulse and throb. Then each one sprang horribly to life as a writhing green serpent.

Athena was out of control! Frozen or not, I had to do something. I shut my eyes, took a deep breath, and called upon the red-hot heat of my Underworld kingdom. Warmth began to flow up through the soles of my feet and into my body. The temperature of my ichor rose, getting hot, hot, hotter. . . .

Athena chanted on:

> *"You're growing wings that are hard and shiny,*
> *And tails with spikes are sprouting out of your—"*

"STOP!" I cried.

Say Cheese, MEDUSA!

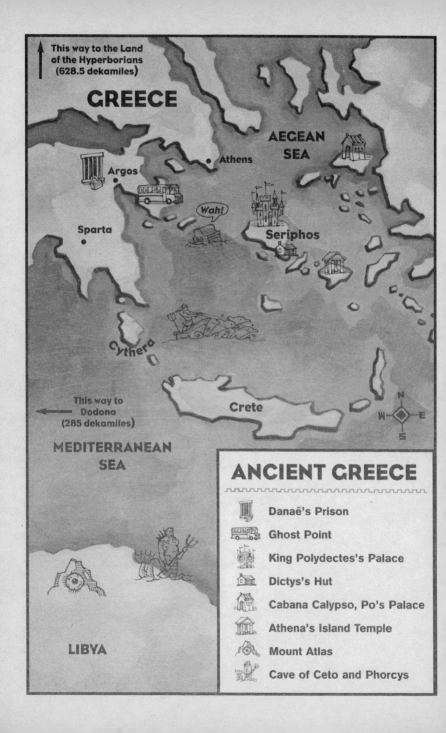

Say Cheese, MEDUSA!

By
Kate McMullan

Illustrated by
David LaFleur

SCHOLASTIC INC.
New York Toronto London Auckland Sydney
Mexico City New Delhi Hong Kong Buenos Aires

ISBN 0-439-54088-7

12 11 10 9 8 7 6 5 4 3 2   3 4 5 6 7 8/0

Printed in the U.S.A.   40

First Scholastic printing, March 2003

For Michael Steiner,
who never has a bad snake day

꜊꜊꜊꜊꜊꜊꜊

Heaps of combustible thank offerings to Susan Chang,
Lisa Holton, Angus Killick, Tara Lewis,
Maria Padilla, Andrea Davis Pinkney,
and all the other myth-o-maniacs at Hyperion

Prologue

Greetings from the Underworld! It's me, Hades, back again to tell you the truth, the whole truth, and nothing but the truth about a Greek myth. Why do I think you might not know the truth, you ask? I'll spell it out for you in just four letters: Z–E–U–S.

My little brother Zeus is King of the Gods. He's also King of the Whoppers. Lies slide off his tongue as if it were greased with butter. Big lies, little lies, white lies, red–yellow–and–blue polka-dotted lies. He's a real myth-o-maniac—old Greek-speak for "big fat liar." And when Zeus decided to "fix up"

The Big Fat Book of Greek Myths, all he did was add one big fat lie after another.

Just look at what he did to the story of Medusa. Go on, read it right from the pages of *The Big Fat Book of Greek Myths* for yourself:

Medusa was a Gorgon, a winged monster with hissing serpents for hair. Anyone who looked upon her face was turned to stone.

Perseus, bold son of the brave and mighty Zeus, waited until Medusa fell asleep, then cut off her horrible head.

How like a son of Zeus to sneak up on his victim while she's asleep! But it didn't happen that way at all. Perseus never hacked off any Gorgon's head. Medusa is alive and well and, last I heard, she was running a popular seaside spa. She wasn't born with serpents sprouting out of her head, either. Those snakes were Athena's idea. Here, let me tell you the story of Medusa. You know you'll always get the truth from me, Hades.

No kidding!

Chapter I

THE CHEESE STANDS ALONE

It all started the very first time my queen, Persephone, had to go back up to earth to do her goddess-of-spring thing. "Hades!" she called. "Come help me close these suitcases!"

I headed for the bedroom with my III-headed pooch, Cerberus, at my heels. I stopped at the door. The room was filled with dozens of large overstuffed suitcases. Not one of them looked as if it would close. Ever!

"Sit on that one, will you, Hades?" Persephone pointed. "Bounce up and down a bit."

I did. Me, King of the Underworld. It was very undignified.

"Bounce harder, Hades," said Persephone. "Good. Got it!"

Persephone is not a goddess who travels light. She'd spent an entire week packing her dozens of robes and tunics. Not to mention handbags, scarves, headbands, and girdles (old-speak for "belts"). But it was her oodles of sandals that put her over the edge, luggage-wise. My dog and I both had to sit on the lids of all those bulging suitcases before she could snap them shut.

"Thanks, Cerbie," Persephone said when the last lock finally clicked. She patted all three of his heads. "Thanks, Hades." She gave my head a pat, too.

Cerberus wagged his stumpy tail. With his triple brain power, he'd figured out that all those suitcases meant Persephone was going bye-bye. He's a one-god dog and likes nothing better than having me all to himself.

Persephone had promised to go up to earth every spring. Her mother, Demeter, is the goddess of agriculture. Wheat, corn, alfalfa sprouts—you name it—Demeter is in charge of making it grow. When Persephone told her mom she wanted to marry me and become Queen of the Underworld, Demeter had a fit. She swore an unbreakable oath on the River Styx that if Persephone lived in the Underworld, all growing things on earth would die. Well, Mother Earth—my Granny Gaia—wasn't about to put up with *that*! There was a big court battle, and at last it was decided that Persephone could only be my part-time queen.

Now, for three months of the year, Persephone lives with me in the Underworld. True to her word, Demeter stops tending the plants on earth and they die. You mortals call this time winter. Then, each year on March XXI, Persephone returns to earth to bring the spring. And she stays for nine months to help her mom. Then on December XXI, she comes back to me. You may think this is a strange arrangement. But for Persephone and me, it works just fine.

"Here, Hades." Persephone handed me a small wrapped box. "I bought you a little going-away present."

"No kidding." I tore off the paper and opened it. "A wallet!" I said, trying to hide my disappointment. "Oh, P-phone, you shouldn't have."

"It's not just any old wallet, Hades," Persephone said. "I had it monogrammed. See?"

I flipped it over. Sure enough, gold letters were stamped into the leather: K.H.R.O.T.U.

I looked up, puzzled. "Khro-tu?"

"King Hades, Ruler of the Underworld." Persephone picked up the big hourglass I keep on my dresser and handed it to me. "Put this in the wallet."

"You're kidding, right?" I said. "That thing is huge."

Persephone gave me one of her looks, so I opened the wallet. To my surprise, it grew as I held it, and the hourglass slipped easily inside. Then the wallet returned to its original size, right before my eyes.

"Wow!" I exclaimed. "How does it do that?"

Persephone shrugged. "It's magical," she said. "I ordered it from the Nymphs of the North Catalog. It expands to hold whatever you want to carry.

Then it shrinks down again so you can put it in your pocket."

"Thank you so much, Phoney, honey!" I said. And then it hit me. I hadn't gotten her anything. "Um, and about your, uh, gift—"

"Oh, stop, Hades," said Persephone. "I know you didn't get me a present. I wanted to surprise you, that's all. But, if you *really* want to, you can take me to dinner tonight at the Underworld Grill."

"You're on!" I said.

"Great." Persephone smiled. "We have an VIII o'clock reservation. And after dinner, you can take me to the concert in Elysium. Blue Cheese Blues is playing. They are so awesome!"

We had a good time.

First thing the next morning, I hitched my steeds, Harley and Davidson, to my biggest chariot and drove Persephone up to earth. I took her right to the door of the little apartment she'd rented in Athens for the spring season, and carried in her bags. They weighed a dekaton! By the time I'd finished, I'd worked up quite a drosis (old Greek-speak for "god sweat").

"Bye, Hades," Persephone said, giving me a hug. "I'll miss you!"

"Bye, P-phone!" I said. "See you next weekend!"

I drove back to the Underworld then. Charon ferried me across the River Styx, and I dropped the usual gold coin into his eager palm.

"Oh, and Lord Hades?" Charon said, as I led Harley and Davidson off his boat. "I hear there's a little problem over at Motel Styx."

Motel Styx is the temporary quarters for ghosts who've just arrived in the Underworld. When I rode over to check it out, I found that every toilet in the place was overflowing. Little problem? Ha! The new ghosts were howling and complaining. Some had even trashed their rooms in protest. It took me the rest of the day to get the plumbing ghosts over there to get the mess mopped up.

At last I headed back to my palace, Villa Pluto. I'd been working so hard all day, I hadn't had time to miss Persephone. But when I walked through the palace door, it hit me. Persephone wasn't there. And she wouldn't be back for months. I sighed as I headed down the hall with Cerbie.

"Uh-oh," Tisi exclaimed when I walked into the den. She stared at me with her fierce red eyes. "Someone is feeling very sorry for himself tonight."

"Okay, I miss Persephone," I said. I plopped down in my La-Z-God recliner with a chilled Necta-Cola and cranked up the footrest. "So, how about we order a pizza and watch a little wrestling?"

Tisi shook her head. The dozens of snakes that sprang from her scalp began hissing softly. "Meg, Alec, and I have a full schedule of avenging ahead of us tonight." (Tisi and her sisters are Furies, whose job it is to punish the wicked.)

"Plus, we have to undo a punishment," she added. She stretched one glossy black wing and then the other in preparation for her flight up to earth. "Remember that young mortal in Thebes I told you about?"

"The one who wouldn't help his mother bring the goats in from pasture?" I asked.

"That's the one." Tisi nodded. "Last week we gave him the Red Eye. We hypnotized him and made him think he was a goat. He was so funny, capering and trotting around with the herd. Even his mother thought so. But enough is enough. Tonight we'll go and bring him back to himself. Gotta run, Hades. Toodle-oo!"

I waved as Tisi left. "Well, Cerbie," I said. "It's just you and me tonight, boy."

Cerberus didn't answer. I looked down and saw that he'd fallen asleep at my feet.

"Make that just me," I muttered. Feeling very much alone, I clicked on the TV. A cheerful announcer was saying, "And for a fifty-drachma pledge, we'll send you the official 'Hugs' Python tote bag!"

Oh, no! I'd forgotten it was fund-raising week on the Wrestling Channel. All matches were on hold until they reached their goal.

"Or for a pledge of two hundred drachmas"—a picture of Hugs flashed onto the screen showing the snake wearing a silver wrestling belt—"we'll send you a signed copy of Hugs's brand-new auto-biography, *Squeeze Play*."

I'm not a Hugs fan, but my little brother, Poseidon, is crazy for the snake. Po's the ruler of the seas. At that time, he was going through a wild party-god phase. He'd put blue streaks in his hair and was wearing one golden sea-horse earring. He was always racing around in his coral-red sea chariot convertible, trying to wow the sea goddesses.

But still, Po was good company. For years, it had just been the two of us, growing up together down in Dad's belly. That's why, of all my brothers and sisters, Po's the one I'm closest to. I decided to give him a call.

We gods have had phones and other high-tech gizmos for centuries, long before you mortals. But recently, Demeter had invented a teeny little portable phone. She'd done it for only one reason— to keep track of Persephone. But most of us gods got the little phones soon after. I hit the number of Po's island palace on my memory dial.

"Hey, Po," I said when he picked up. "It's me, Hades."

"Hades, you old dog," said Po. "What's going on?"

"Not much," I said. "Persephone had to go back to earth. You free to have dinner?"

"Free as a fish, big bro," said Po. "Come on over!"

"Be right there." I hopped out of my La-Z-God. Cerbie was still out, with two mouths snoring. "See you, pup!"

I hurried to the bedroom to get my Helmet of Darkness. It was a gift from my Cyclopes uncles, and I never leave home without it. When I put it on, *POOF!* I vanish. (At least that's what happens XCV percent of the time. The other V percent, the helmet spews sparks and shorts out.)

I slipped the helmet into my wallet and watched, amazed, as it shrank down again to pocket size. I had to hand it to Persephone. She'd gotten me an incredibly useful gift. What could I get her, I wondered, as I slipped the wallet into my robe pocket. I clipped my lunx (old Greek-speak for "flashlight") onto my girdle and headed for the stable. There, I hitched Harley and Davidson to my small II-seater chariot, and galloped up to earth.

We gods can travel instantly to most places in the cosmos. We simply chant an astro-traveling spell, and *ZIP!* we're there. (Where do you think ZIP codes come from?) But astro-traveling doesn't work to get us to the Underworld. It takes most immortals nine days to travel between earth and my kingdom. Even I, the king of the place, have to travel the old-fashioned way—by foot, donkey, or chariot. Luckily, I know a super shortcut, and I got up to earth that day in under two hours.

I galloped to Phaeton's Chariot Garage, outside Athens, and parked in the short-term lot. Then I chanted the spell and *ZIP!* Seconds later, my feet touched down on the sands of Po's island. I headed up the crushed-oyster-shell walk to Cabana Calypso, Po's palace, which is built entirely of seashells. One of Po's sea nymphs let me in.

"Your brother is dressing, King Hades," she said.

I thanked her and headed down the hallway. "Po?" I called.

"In the bathroom, Hades!" he answered.

I walked back, and found Po, grinning into his shell-bedecked mirror.

"Hey, hey, Hades!" he said, slapping on way too much Sea Breeze cologne. "Are you ready to party the night away, big brother?"

"What are you talking about, Po?" I said. "We're just having dinner."

"Don't drosis it, Hades," Po said. "We're still having dinner. Only now we're being joined by three of the most gorgeous young moon goddesses this side of Olympus." His sea-blue eyes lit up. "I mean, they are lookers, Hades. Long silky hair, nice—"

"Hold it!" I said. "I'm not up for a party tonight, Po!"

"You will be, big bro," said Po. He grabbed my elbow and began pulling me down the hallway with him. "First we'll go tubing. You won't believe my new dolphins, Hades. They're speed demons! They go about two hundred dekameters a second. It's like flying!"

I try never to travel on water, because I get seasick. Even rowboats make me feel queasy. But Po dragged me down to his dock and yanked me into the sea chariot beside him. A big cooler sat on the backseat, along with the inflated sea monster's bladder that Po used for tubing.

"Oh, and guess who else is joining us, bro?" said Po. "Zeus."

"Zeus?" I cried. "Why didn't you tell me?"

"I just did." Po revved up his dolphins. "Lighten up, Hades!" he shouted as we started bumping madly over the waves. "The three of us haven't done anything fun together since our road trip down to the Underworld when we sprang the Cyclopes from jail."

I couldn't yell over the noise—Po's new dolphins were real screechers—and with so much spray hitting my face, so I only nodded. Spending an evening with Po in his party-god mode had its downside. But spending an evening with Zeus? That would be torture! I'd have to listen to the old myth-o-maniac's endless bragging, his everlasting lies. What could be worse?

Then Po yelled, "We're meeting Zeus at Athena's brand-new temple! It's only been open a couple of days. I thought it would be a fun spot for a moonlight picnic."

"What?" I cried. "Have you lost your mind? Athena only allows mortals bearing really spectacular sacrifices to set foot in her temples. She considers this new temple to be the most sacred of them all! She'd go nuts if she thought we were going there for a picnic!"

"I know, I know!" Po yelled back. "That's why it'll be so much fun!"

Chapter II

RICOTTA GET OUTTA HERE!

Po's new dolphins hydroplaned over the waves. Islands went by in a blur. All I could do was hold on tight and try not to throw up.

Plus, Po's idea of a joke had made me break out in a cold drosis. If Athena caught anyone having a picnic at her new temple, she'd go ballistic. But if she caught Po? There was no telling what she'd do. She and Po had hated each other ever since a certain contest. . . .

Centuries ago, some crafty mortals announced that they would name their city after the god who gave them the best gift. Both Po and Athena thought it should be named for them. Po gave his gift first. He banged his trident—his three-pronged spear that looks like a fish fork—on a rock, and water burbled up in a spring. Athena went next. She planted an olive tree.

Lots of mortals said Po's gift of water was better. They wanted to name their city Poseidonville. But other mortals said the tree was better because it gave many gifts: shade from the sun, olives, olive oil, and firewood. The mortals argued back and forth. The arguing made them thirsty, so they bent down to drink from the spring. *Bleeech!* The water was salty, like the sea. So all the mortals quickly agreed to name their city Athens, after Athena.

Ever since then, Po had tried to get even with Athena every chance he got. Athena called Po a sore loser. She couldn't stand him, and she was a champion grudge holder. The two were sworn enemies.

At last, Po slowed his dolphins. Athena's new temple loomed ahead of us, sparkling white in the moonlight. And there was Zeus, standing on the dock. He was pumping a fist in the air. I'd have bet anything that he was chanting, "Party! Party! Party!"

How I wanted to yank my helmet out of my wallet, put it on, and vanish into the salty night air! But if you've got brothers—especially younger brothers—then you know how sometimes you've just got to stick things out, or they'll call you names like "party pooper" or "sad sack" for the rest of your life. And, since Zeus, Po, and I are immortals, I'd have to listen to their taunting basically for-ever.

Po saw Zeus and went for a show-off landing. He sped up his dolphins, and we whizzed toward the island. Just as we were about to crash into it, Po let go of the reins. The dolphins made a tight right turn, but the chariot kept going straight, sliding halfway up on the white sand beach.

"All right!" cried Po, jumping out of the chariot. "Are those dolphins crazy, or what?"

"Go, Po!" said Zeus. "Hades?" he added when he saw me. "Who invited you?"

"Good to see you, too, Zeus," I muttered, stepping onto dry land at last.

"Where are the minor moon goddesses, Po?" said Zeus. "You said they'd be here."

Po looked out to sea. "Here they come. Looks like they borrowed their old man's chariot."

A sea chariot shaped like a crescent moon was heading our way, drawn by a team of giant sea horses. I knew that chariot. It belonged to Phorcys, a wise old sea god who'd gladly given up his power when Po came along to rule the seas. Now I knew which moon goddesses Po was talking about— Phorcys's daughters, Eno, Riley, and Medusa. They were goddess friends of Persephone's, and had been guests at our wedding.

The sea horses stopped in the surf. The moon goddesses hopped out of the chariot, and began wading to shore. They ruled over the moon's pull on the ocean tides and weren't afraid to get their feet wet.

"Hey, moon ladies!" called Po, waving his trident.

"Po?" called Medusa. "Can you give us a ride home later? Dad wants us to send the chariot back."

"No problemo!" Po replied.

Medusa whistled to the sea horses, and they took off again.

Po elbowed me. "Check out Medusa's hair, Hades," he said. "Gorgeous, huh?"

I nodded. All three goddesses had beautiful silky hair. Eno was a blonde, and Riley, a redhead. Medusa's hair was black and so shiny that it reflected the silvery moonlight.

"Hey, Hades!" Medusa called as she reached the shore. Then she stopped suddenly, looking up at Athena's temple. "I thought you said this was *your* temple, Po."

"Right!" said Po. "Yeah, so how do you like my new temple, anyway?"

"Very nice," said Medusa. "But why is there an owl on the top? Didn't Athena claim the owl as her mascot?"

"Owl?" said Po. "Oh, you mean *that* owl. Yeah, well, uh . . ."

"That's a sea owl," Zeus lied quickly. "Flies sometimes, swims other times. Amazing creature, really."

I couldn't believe my brothers! One was a

myth-o-maniac, and the other went along with his lies. They reminded me of our dad, Cronus, a truly slimy Titan. I took after our mother, Rhea.

"So, who's up for a little high-speed tubing?" called Po.

"We are!" said the goddesses.

Po whistled for his dolphins, and they came leaping through the surf almost to the shore. Po pushed his sea chariot into the shallow water, and hitched up his team again.

"I can only take three at a time," said Po. "Who wants to go?"

"Me!" said Zeus.

"Go on," Medusa told her sisters. "I'll go next round."

Eno, Riley, and Zeus waded out to the chariot, jumped in, and they all sped off.

"What a nice surprise to see you, Hades," Medusa said, sitting down on the dock. "Is Persephone around?"

I shook my head. "She has to work. You know, it's spring, and she's the goddess of it. I'll go see her on weekends. What's happening with you?"

"Well, I just got back from visiting my three older sisters," Medusa said.

"I didn't know you had any other sisters," I said.

"I didn't either," said Medusa. "But the other night, Mom happened to mention something about the Gray Sisters, and I got her to tell me all about them. Turns out they have some, um . . . unfortunate physical characteristics."

"Oddballs, huh?" I said.

"Very odd." Medusa nodded. "Mom said it gave her the willies to look at them, so she sent them off to live on a mountaintop."

"My grandpa, Sky Daddy, did the same thing with some of his kids." I shook my head. "Three of his sons had one big eye in the middle of their foreheads. And three others had fifty heads and one hundred arms apiece. Sky Daddy couldn't believe his children were such misfits, so he hurled them down to Tartarus, the fiery pit in what's now my kingdom, and had them locked up in jail."

"That stinks," said Medusa. "It's so unfair to judge gods or goddesses—or even mortals—by the way they look. Mom feels bad about what she did.

She agreed to let me tell everyone in the family about the Gray Sisters. Now they'll have plenty of visitors on their mountaintop. And maybe some day they'll come out of hiding."

"That'd be great," I said. "Po, Zeus, and I rescued our uncles. They live down in the Underworld now. I see them all the time and don't even notice their looks."

"Every family has its share of strange ducks, I guess," said Medusa. "I tried to talk Eno and Riley into visiting the Gray Sisters, but all they ever want to do is stay around here and go to Po's parties."

"Weren't *you* the one dancing all night with Po at our wedding reception?" I said.

Medusa smiled. "Po's persistent, I'll say that for him. And I love to dance."

I liked talking to Medusa, but at the same time, I kept a sharp lookout for Athena. She made me nervous. Athena wasn't like the rest of us gods. For one thing, she wasn't born in the usual way. Instead, she sprang, fully-grown, out of Zeus's head, wearing a helmet and armor and waving a spear. She came ready-made to be goddess of war! She had such a temper. The least little thing could set her off. And she absolutely forbid any fooling around near her temples.

Once some naiads, little water nymphs, were in a river beside one of her temples, swimming and frolicking. Athena got so angry that she blasted them with a dog-head spell. Instantly, those nymphs grew muzzles, wet black noses, and long floppy ears. And, since Athena had tricked the muse Calliope into teaching her to deliver her curses in verses, which made them incredibly powerful, the poor naiads still have dog heads to this day. I didn't want to imagine what sort of curse Athena might utter if she found Medusa and me yakking in her sacred spot.

At last we heard dolphins screeching, and Po landed his chariot. He hoisted the cooler out of the backseat. "We're hungry!" he said. "Who's ready for some eats?"

"Me!" cried Zeus.

Riley ran off down the beach. The rest of us sat down around a cloth Po had spread out on the sand. I handed out Necta-Colas while Po passed around a big platter of sushios, a little delicacy he had invented made of raw bits of fish wrapped in seaweed. Medusa and Eno helped themselves to several pieces each.

But Zeus growled, "What's this stuff? Looks like bait."

For once, I agreed with Zeus.

"It's sushios," said Po. "The deluxe platter! Tuna-ambrosia rolls. The works!"

"Is this all you brought?" asked Zeus.

It was. Zeus and I had to content ourselves with our Necta-Colas.

"Tah-dah!" Riley called from down the beach. We all turned, and saw that she'd sculpted a dolphin out of the sparkling white sand.

"Wow," said Po. "That's life-size!"

"Anybody can make a fish," scoffed Zeus. "Now make something for the king of the gods!"

"Easy!" Riley said, and proved it by quickly sculpting a giant T-bolt. Then she came over and finished off the sushios.

"So, Po," I said, jumping to my feet. "Ready to call it a night?"

"Sit down, you dolt," said Zeus.

"Don't go, Hades," said Eno. She held up a small kamara (old Greek-speak for "camera"). "I want to take a group shot with the temple in the background."

"No!" I cried. The *last* thing we needed was absolute proof that we'd been picnicking at Athena's temple.

But Eno popped up and scurried off toward the water. Then she turned and pointed her kamara at us. "Smile, Po!" she said. "Smile, Riley! Look at the birdie, Zeus! Lighten up, Hades!"

I made a feeble attempt.

"Say cheese, Medusa!"

Click!

"Got it!" said Eno. "If it's any good, I'll send you gods copies."

"No copies!" I yelled. Everyone looked at me as if I were some sort of nutcase. "I mean, why go to the trouble, Eno? Okay, it's late. Time to go home."

"Hades, stop fussing!" Zeus growled. "We just got here. Why, the moon goddesses haven't even had a tour of Poseidon's new temple yet." He gave me a wicked wink and sprang to his feet. "Riley! Come! Let me show you the temple. It's magnificent."

"Wait!" I cried. I had to keep my brothers out of Athena's temple. "Why don't we go visit one of the other islands around here." I pointed. "Look! That one over there. It's deserted. We could be the first gods ever to set foot on it."

"Big whoopie," said Zeus. "Come on, ladies! Po's temple awaits."

My mind flashed back to the time our mom, Rhea, had taken me, her firstborn, aside. She'd asked me to keep an eye on my siblings, to make sure they stayed out of trouble. Had she known at the time how impossibly hard this would be? I had five brothers and sisters. Hestia behaved herself. But the other four were magnets for trouble.

Eno grabbed her kamara. "Let's go!" she cried.

"Coming, Medusa?" said Zeus.

"No thanks," said Medusa. "I'm enjoying sitting here talking to your brother."

"Hades?" Zeus looked confused. "You *like* talking to him?"

Medusa laughed. "Of course," she said, and it warmed my heart to hear it.

Zeus shrugged. "All right. Last one up to the temple is a rotin oion [old Greek slang for 'rotten egg']!"

Zeus, Eno, and Riley raced up the temple steps.

"You were just waiting for *me* to show you my temple, right, Medusa?" said Po.

"Not really, Po," she said. "If you've seen one temple, you've seen them all."

"Not this temple," said Po. "It's incredible. Sculpture all over the walls. I promise, you've never seen anything like it. Let me give you a little tour."

Medusa rolled her eyes. "Okay, Po," she said, standing up. She looked back over her shoulder at me. "Come on, Hades."

I shook my head. I figured I'd stay put and keep an eye out for Athena. If she showed up, maybe I could keep her busy on the beach until everybody had a chance to get out of the temple.

Po and Medusa started up the stairs. I started pacing. A temple tour would take five minutes, tops. After all, the inside of a temple is a simple affair. There's one altar where mortals put room-temperature offerings, such as an ear of corn, a sheaf of wheat, or a nice cheese ball. A second altar holds offerings to be set on fire—smoked turkey, lamb burgers, toasted cheese sandwiches—and has a chimney over it for channeling the sweet-smelling smoke up to Mount Olympus.

But time dragged on. What, I wondered, could Po be showing Medusa that was taking so long? I counted to fifty, then ran up the temple stairs myself.

I stepped through the arched doorway of Athena's temple. The walls were covered in carvings of olive trees, a little reminder of her victory over Po. On the ceiling, various immortals brandished spears, axes, swords, and other weapons of war. Athena had clearly spent a bundle on the decor.

Zeus, Eno, and Riley stood at the far end of the room by the burnt-offering table. Zeus was bragging and the goddesses were giggling. Po and Medusa were sitting on the other offering table, looking up at the ceiling sculptures. Right next to Po was some scrumptious-looking sliced salami that a mortal had left for Athena. I thought about taking some—that

Necta-Cola hadn't exactly filled me up—but quickly thought better of it. If Athena ever found out, I'd be toast!

"You'll be able to see it better if you lean a little closer," Po was saying.

"Give it up, Po." Medusa laughed.

"All right, time to go!" I called. "We gotta get out of here!"

Medusa turned and saw me. She opened her mouth. She looked as if she were about to say, "Hey, Hades! Am I ever glad to see you!" Something like that. But she never got the chance.

A sudden flash lit the room. The clang of metal hitting marble made my ichor (old Greek-speak for "god blood") run cold. I made myself turn.

There, in the doorway, stood Athena.

Chapter III

HORRIBLE MUENSTERS!

Athena's gray eyes flashed angrily. "Poseidon! I should have guessed!" she hissed. An owl was perched on her shoulder. It glowered at us too. "What are you doing in my temple?"

No one answered. The sound of flapping wings broke the silence. I glanced up and saw a pigeon fly up the burnt-offering chimney. I didn't even have to look back down to know that when I did, Zeus would be missing. How like him to morph into a pigeon and fly away rather than stick around to face his sizzling-mad daughter!

Athena's face was red. Her helmet glowed with a fierce hot light. "Empty Necta-Cola cans on my porch," she said, poking in Po's direction with her spear. "Half-eaten fish parts! You've been picnicking at my temple!"

Eno's kamara fell from her hand. She and Riley huddled behind Medusa, peeking out from behind her.

I spoke up. "We're sorry, Athena. I know it looks bad. But—"

"Looks bad?" Athena cut me off. "I'll say. And it's about to look a whole lot worse." She fixed her gaze on Medusa. "You, lowly goddess with the dark hair. Who are you?"

"Hoo, hoo?" echoed her owl.

"Medusa," the moon goddess answered, taking a step forward.

"Medusa." Athena nodded slowly. "I've seen you before." She glanced at Po. "She's the one you're always going on and on about, isn't she?"

"Right." Po grinned. "She's the one."

"Medusa," Athena repeated bitterly. "You, who enjoy the attentions of the sea god. You, who arrange picnics at temples where you have no business being. *You* are about to be punished."

"Hold it, Athena," I said. "The picnic wasn't Medusa's idea."

"Quiet!" Athena snapped.

I eyed Po. I gestured for him to speak up, to tell Athena that he was the one with the bright idea of picnicking at her temple. But Po wouldn't meet my gaze.

I tried again. "Athena, Po and I were the ones—"

"Be quiet, Hades," warned Athena. "This is my temple. I have the power here."

"But, Athena—" I began. That was as far as I got. Athena pointed at me and chanted:

"I told you once, I told you twice,
So now I freeze you hard as ice."

I felt a jolt as my ichor turned to ice. I couldn't move a muscle. I couldn't say a word. Athena had zapped me with a freezing curse! Me, a major god! I had no idea her curses in verses were *that* powerful.

Athena smiled, then turned to Po. "Not a word

out of you, Poseidon, or I'll freeze you so fast you won't know what hit you. Now watch while I gorgonize your little girlfriend."

Athena raised her hands toward Medusa and began chanting:

"Hair-proud goddess, vain and haughty,
How you'll wish you'd never been naughty.
How you'll weep for insulting Athena,
Some goddesses are mean, but I'm much meaner!
When you look in a mirror, you'll get shivers and
shakes,
Your long thick hair is now a nest of snakes!"

Instantly, Medusa's hair twisted itself into dozens of long, dark braids. The braids began to pulse and throb. Then each one sprang horribly to life as a writhing green serpent.

Eno and Riley screamed.

"Don't cry," said Athena. "You get some, too!" She pointed a finger at them, and their hair turned to snakes. Eno's were yellow with thin black stripes. Riley's snakes were bright red.

"Hoo, hoo!" Athena's owl hooted triumphantly.

The poor moon goddesses! They needed help. I tried to break out of my icy state, but I was still frozen solid.

Athena wasn't finished. She chanted:

"Don't look now, you've got bulging eyes,
Your teeth have turned to tusks of enormous size!"

Athena pointed at each helpless goddess in turn. Their eyes bugged out. Huge boar's tusks shot from their gums.

After a satisfied smirk, Athena kept going:

"Vile-smelling drool drips from your jaws,
Your skin is scaly, your feet have claws!"

Athena was out of control! Frozen or not, I had to do something.

Athena was powerful, but I was the firstborn of the great gods. I was a power guy myself. And I ruled a kingdom of fire. Of eternal flames and rivers of burning lava. I shut my eyes, took a deep breath, and called upon the red-hot heat of my Underworld kingdom. Warmth began to flow up through the soles of my feet and into my body. The temperature of my ichor rose, getting hot, hot, hotter. . . .

Athena chanted on:

"You're growing wings that are hard and shiny,
  And tails with spikes are sprouting out of your—"

"STOP!" I cried.

"Hoo?" the owl hooted in surprise.

Yes! Fire had won over ice! I'd broken out of Athena's spell.

"Hades! How dare you?" Athena cried. "I'm not finished here!"

"Oh, yes, you are, Athena," I said.

Eno and Riley looked at each other and burst into tears. Medusa put her arms around her sisters' shoulders, trying to comfort them. Who wouldn't be upset? The once lovely goddesses now had snakes for hair, bulbous eyes, tusks, scales, claws, and wings. I wished I could have spoken up sooner, but at least I'd kept them from sprouting tails.

"Oh, they're monsters!" Po moaned. "Horrible monsters."

Po's words seemed to cheer Athena. She tilted her helmeted head to the side, studying her creations. Then she muttered a few words to her owl. The bird rose from her shoulder and swooped down to where Eno's kamara had fallen. The bird picked it up in its talons, and flew back with it to his mistress.

"Thank you, Hoo," said Athena. She pointed the kamara at the Gorgons.

Click!

Athena laughed. "Now you can remember this moment forever, monsters!"

"Call us what you like, Athena," Medusa said. "But we know who we are. We are the daughters of Phorcys, a wise old god of the sea. We will survive, for we are also wise!"

I admired Medusa for standing up to Athena. But when she claimed to be wise, I braced myself. After all, Athena *is* the official goddess of wisdom. Under the circumstances, it wasn't a good idea for Medusa to step on her goddess turf.

"Wise, are you, Medusa?" Athena shrieked. "Not wise enough to know when to keep your mouth shut!" She pointed to Medusa and began to chant again:

"Medusa, here's a curse for you alone,
Whoever sees your face shall be turned to stone!
Gods or mortals, there's no place to hide,
One peek at you, and they're petrified!"

Po clapped his hands over his eyes. He wasn't taking any chances. I looked away too. I felt like a traitor. But I wanted to help the Gorgons, and I couldn't do that if I got turned to stone.

"Your curse is weak, Athena," said Medusa. "My sisters are gazing at my face right now and they haven't turned to stone."

"Oh, so you want them to turn to stone?" cried Athena. "No problem!"

"Quick, sisters!" cried Medusa. "Fly!"

I heard flapping again, but this time of great, powerful wings as the Gorgons flew up and circled over our heads.

"I'll get you, Gorgons!" Athena cried after them.

"Out of the temple, Eno!" Medusa called, flapping her wings. "Riley, flee, quickly!"

"Tails with spikes!" Athena screamed. "Tails with scales! Tails so heavy your wings won't lift you off the ground! You'll have to crawl like lizards!"

As Athena ranted, the Gorgons swooped out through the arched doorway of the temple and vanished into the night.

Chapter IV

CHEESE ALL THAT

It was quiet after the Gorgons had flown. Very quiet.

At last Athena spoke. "You are never to set foot in my temple again, Po."

"Right," said Po.

"The same goes for you, Hades," Athena added.

I nodded. That was one command I'd be happy to obey.

"I will find those Gorgons," Athena said. "And when I do, it won't be pretty." She eyed Po. "Now go. Both of you! And take your fishy picnic leavings with you. And here—" She tossed Eno's kamara to me. "A picture like the one I just took might win a prize!"

Po and I turned and ran down the steps. I picked up our trash from the beach while Po whistled to his dolphins. Seconds later we were zooming over the water.

"Po!" I cried as we sped away from Athena's temple. "How could you let those poor moon goddesses take the blame for you? They didn't even know that it was Athena's temple. If anyone should have been punished, it's you!"

"I know it!" Po shouted over the dolphins. "I feel awful! But once Athena got going on that whole Gorgon thing, it was too late to help the moon goddesses. So there wasn't much point in me confessing."

"Whatever," I said. "But we have to find Medusa and her sisters before Athena does. We have to get them a place to hide!"

"Hmmmm." Po grew thoughtful. "This might be a job for SNIPP."

"And that would be, what?" I asked.

"It's part of SNIT," Po said.

"Po! What are you talking about?"

"I'll explain in a sec, bro," said Po. "Right now I'll bet the Gorgons are flying to their parents' cave in Libya. If I get my team up to full speed, we can probably make it there before they do." He gave an earsplitting whistle and pulled on the reins. His dolphins veered to the left, and turned up the speed.

Once again I found myself being jolted over the waves. Only this time we were going ten times faster than before. I was beyond seasick. The dolphins weren't squeaking now. They put everything they had into racing toward Libya.

"SNIT is my Sea Nymph Intelligence Team!" Po shouted as we hurtled across the ocean. "Anything I want to know, they can find out. They run SNIPP, the Sea Nymph Island Protection Program. If the Gorgons go into the program, they'll be given new identities—new names, new clothes, the works. Plus a pair of sea nymph agents to guard them XXIV/VII. No one—not even Athena—will be able to find them."

"New names and clothes aren't exactly going to disguise the Gorgons," I pointed out.

"Don't be too sure, Hades," Po said. "My sea nymphs are very resourceful."

When we reached the Libyan coast, Po steered into an inlet. At its far end was Ceto and Phorcys's cave. There, we found Eno and Riley trying to explain to their horrified parents how Athena had cursed them, and that she was coming after them. They were crying and drooling and carrying on— and who could blame them? But Medusa sat calmly in a corner of the cave, her arms folded across her chest. She had wrapped layers of seaweed around her face as a precaution, to keep from turning her parents to stone. Her head snakes sprouted from above the seaweed. She looked like an exotic piece of Po's sushios.

Phorcys turned toward us as we came ashore. On top, he looked like any god, but from the waist down, he was all fishtail. "Ah, Lord Poseidon, Lord Hades," Phorcys said. "Have you gods come to help my poor daughters?"

"We can't undo the curse," Po said. "Sorry."

"Oh, the snakes are a nice touch," said Ceto, who looked pretty much like a large sea snake herself. "An orthodontist could work on those tusks, and that would take care of the drooling." She smiled encouragingly at her daughters. "Listen, there are probably some nice young Gorgon guys around who'll be crazy for your new look."

"Mom!" groaned Eno.

"This isn't about getting us husbands!" said Riley.

Po spoke up then. "SNIPP may be able to help," he said. "It's a protection program. If you go into it, sea nymph agents will pick you up. They'll blindfold you and take you to their secret training island. Not even I, god of the seas, know where it is. No one will know where you are," he said with a nod to Ceto and Phorcys. "There, you'll be given new identities. When you leave, you'll begin new lives."

"Eno, you and Riley must go into this program," Medusa said through the seaweed mask. "It's the only way you'll be safe from Athena."

"But what about you, Medusa?" I asked. "Athena is out to get you most of all."

"I'll join my sisters later," Medusa said. "I have a few things to take care of first."

"Like revenge?" Po asked.

The seaweed-draped head nodded.

"Oh, no, my daughter!" Phorcys cried. "You will never get the best of Athena. She is a powerful Olympian. Her father is Zeus! Against such a foe, you cannot hope to win."

"Listen to your father, Medusa," Ceto said. "Who knows what sorts of interesting types are being flipped over in SNIPP? You could meet someone and begin your new lives together!"

"Great, Mom," Medusa muttered.

"Once you're safe, then you can think of revenge," Po added. "I'll help you, Medusa. I have a few scores to settle with Athena myself."

"Tell me, Po," said Medusa. "What did I do to bring down Athena's wrath? I'd only seen her once or twice in my life. It makes no sense!"

"I know it," said Po.

Medusa shook her snaky head. "Athena is crazed. She's berserk! She's over the top!"

"She's all that," Po agreed. "The trouble is,

Athena doesn't know the meaning of fun. Why, she came to one of my parties once and never even took her helmet off. She's a total party pooper. Did I tell you about the time she—"

"She's coming after Medusa and her sisters, Po!" I said, cutting him off. "No time for stories now." I turned to Medusa. "Play it safe and smart, Medusa. Go with your sisters."

"Please, daughter," said Phorcys. "Listen to Lord Hades!"

"Do it for me!" said Ceto.

"But I can turn anyone who looks at me to stone," said Medusa. "Even Athena. I don't need protection!"

"Then go for the sake of your sisters," said Ceto. "They need you to look after them."

Now Ceto sounded like *my* mom! And her plea worked just as well as Mom's would have.

Medusa heaved a sigh beneath her seaweed mask. "All right," she said. "I'll go."

"I'll call SNIPP Headquarters." Po pulled out his phone. I was glad to hear him begin speaking in Sea Nymphese. Hardly anyone understands this little-spoken undersea language. And the fewer clues to lead Athena to Medusa and her sisters, the better.

"They're on their way," Po said, hanging up.

"I'll help you pack, girls," offered Ceto. "Sounds as if you'd better take most everything."

Unlike Persephone, the Gorgons traveled light. They packed quickly. And no sooner were the strings of their waterproof duffels drawn up tight than two agents from SNIPP arrived. They swam into the inlet, surfacing just beyond the waves.

"Agent Smithias reporting, Lord Poseidon!" called one of the sea nymphs.

"Agent Jonesias reporting, sir!" called the other. "Those entering the protection program, please step into the water."

Po and I said good-bye to Medusa, Eno, and Riley.

"I'll keep in touch," Po told Medusa.

The seaweed-head nodded.

The Gorgons hugged their parents, then waded into the surf. Ceto waved a handkerchief after them. Then she used it to dab at the salty tears running down her cheeks. We watched the sea nymphs blindfold the Gorgons. They all disappeared beneath the water's surface.

We said good-bye to Ceto and Phorcys.

"This wasn't the night I had in mind," said Po glumly as he got into his sea chariot.

He took off. I astro-traveled back to Phaeton's, picked up my chariot, and headed for home. The whole way there, I kept wondering about Athena. Why had she singled out Medusa for her worst wrath?

By the time I reached the Underworld, it was late. Charon, the old chisler, charged me a sky-high after-hours rate to ferry me across the Styx. So I was glad to see my loyal dog Cerberus waiting for me just inside the Gates. When he saw my chariot coming, he ran to greet me. "Whoa, Harley! Whoa, Davidson!" I called. They stopped, and Cerbie leaped into my lap and gave me the old triple licking. "Yes, you're my good old boy, boy, boy."

I steered my steeds for Villa Pluto. As I passed the entrance to Cave LIV, I reined in my steeds.

(There are far too many caves in my kingdom for me to name them all, so I numbered them.) LIV was the perfect spot to pick up an I've-missed-you gift for Persephone.

Cerbie and I headed into the cave. Did I mention that, in addition to being king of the Underworld, I'm also god of wealth? Well, I am. All the caves in my kingdom are loaded with gold, silver, and precious gems. I turned on my lunx and shone it onto small rubies and emeralds sparkling in the walls. But for the stone I had in mind, I'd have to go far deeper into the cave.

I kept walking. The path inside Cave LIV grew steep. I trudged up it, climbing higher and higher. Finally I stopped to catch my breath. I don't know who was panting harder, Cerbie or me. Suddenly Cerbie started growling and ran off.

"Cerbie!" I called. "Wait!" I flashed my lunx ahead on the path. Cerbie was nowhere to be seen. I took off running. "Where are you, pup?" When I caught up to him, I found him sitting in front of something that looked like a wall of brass. He was barking his heads off. What *was* this thing?

I walked along the wall until I came to a corner. I kept going until I had turned three more corners. It was a large cube. I'd never seen anything like it before. I knocked on it. *Bang! Bang!* After a moment, I heard a faint *Bang! Bang!* in reply.

Someone—or something—had knocked back!

I cupped my hands to my mouth and called, "Hellooooo in there!"

I put my ear to the box and was shocked to hear a muffled reply. Cerbie pricked up all six ears.

This was too bizarre. I knew I couldn't open the box by myself, so I pulled out my phone and punched in the Cyclopes' number.

"Uncle Shiner?" I said. "It's me, Hades. Can you and your brothers get over to Cave LIV on the double? And bring your tools!"

While I waited for my uncles, I searched the walls until I found a perfectly round emerald that I knew Persephone would love. I slipped it into my pocket just as the Cyclopes arrived.

"Salutations, Hades," said Uncle Shiner.

"Hey, Uncles!" I said, squinting into the bright beams of the miner's lights they wore strapped to their foreheads above their great single eyes. "Look what Cerbie found."

The three Cyclopes walked around the cube, inspecting it, as I had done.

"Something's in there," I told them. "I heard it knock. I think I heard it grunt, too."

"It must be a monster of some ferocity," Uncle Shiner said. "That seems the most likely motive for someone to secure it inside a metal prison."

Thunderer and Lightninger nodded in agreement.

"Can you open it?" I asked.

"Absolutely." Uncle Shiner nodded. "But perhaps it would be best not to release such a terrible beast."

Uncle Shiner had a point. What if there was a giant lava-spewing monster like Typhon in there? I shuddered, thinking back to the time Zeus and I had battled the huge fiend before we trapped it under Mount Etna. I didn't want to let anything like that loose in my kingdom. But I knew I wouldn't sleep a wink that night if I didn't find out what was inside that box. "If it's a really scary monster," I said, "we'll drive it back inside and seal up the hole."

Uncle Shiner shrugged. "You're the monarch," he said. "Now, stand away, Hades. And be prepared to face a formidable opponent!"

I stepped back. I figured that if worse came to worse, I'd put on my Helmet of Darkness, scoop up Cerbie and make a run for it.

Uncle Shiner turned to his brothers. "Thunderer and Lightninger, ready the brass blasters. Don your orb protection devices. We shall commence the opening of this mysterious container."

The Cyclopes pulled small blowtorches from their packs. They put on their safety uni-goggles and began blasting away at the cube. In a few minutes, they had made a large, rectangular cut in the metal.

"Cease!" said Uncle Shiner. "Thunderer, procure drilling implement. Lightninger, obtain hinges and double-sided doorknob. I, personally, shall oversee the installation of the knocker."

Working at great speed, the Cyclopes smiths turned their cut into a proper door.

"Now, let us see what transpires." Uncle Shiner picked up the knocker and banged three times on the door.

Lightninger and Thunderer stood with their brass blasters pointed at the box. Uncle Shiner held a hammer ready. Cerbie pressed up against my leg, trembling. All eyes were on that door.

Slowly, the doorknob began to turn.

"Steady, brothers!" whispered Uncle Shiner.

The door opened slightly. Inch by inch it creaked loudly forward on its hinges.

"Sorry," muttered Thunderer. "I should have oiled them."

Suddenly the door swung wide open.

And there stood the formidable opponent.

Chapter V

GRATED!

Our opponent appeared to be a pale young woman holding a baby. She didn't have the telltale glow that we immortals have, so I guessed she had to be a mortal. The mother and baby looked out at us in stunned silence.

"Don't be afraid," I said.

With a god, a III-headed hound, and a couple of blowtorch-wielding Cyclopes staring at her, it was a wonder the poor mortal didn't faint dead away.

"Who . . . who are you?" the mortal whispered.

"I am King Hades, Ruler of the Underworld," I said. "These are my uncles, the Cyclopes. They got you out of there." I nodded toward the cube.

"Oh, are we dead?" she asked.

"No, you're not dead," I assured her. "But who are you? And how did you get here?"

"My name is Danaë, Princess of Argos," said the mortal. "And this is my son, Perseus."

The baby looked about a year old. But mortals age so quickly, it was hard for me to tell.

"My father is King Acrisius of Argos," Danaë continued. "I am his only child. My father desperately wished for a son, so he traveled to—"

Just then baby Perseus spotted Cerberus and gave an earsplitting shriek. He held out both of his pudgy hands and continued to screech in a most horrible manner.

"What's wrong with him?" I shouted over the shrieking. That baby reminded me of someone.

"Perseus has been shut inside that brass cage his whole life and has never seen a dog before!" Danaë shouted back. "I believe he would like to pat your dog, Lord Hades."

I glanced at Cerberus. Not one of his faces looked eager for this to happen. But it seemed rude to say no.

"It's okay, Cerbie," I said. "The baby is just going to give one of your heads a little pat."

Danaë put the baby down beside Cerberus.

"Go on with your story," I said to Danaë.

Danaë nodded. "Some years ago, my father went to the oracle of Delphi. There, he asked a sibyl priestess whether he would ever have a son to inherit his kingdom."

Another shriek came from the floor of the cave. I looked down to see what was wrong with Perseus now, but the baby was entirely happy. He sat astride Cerberus, banging his heels into the poor dog's sides, and shrieking with delight.

"You like the doggie, don't you, Perseus?" exclaimed Danaë.

I bent down and whisked the rowdy baby off Cerbie's back. Perseus looked at me in surprise. Then he opened his mouth and started screaming. I handed him back to his mother.

I gave my dog a pat. "Sorry about that, Cerbie."

Cerberus raised the tops of his lips in a triple sneer.

The baby's cries echoed off the cave walls. I wanted to hear Danaë's story, so I shouted an invitation to come back with me to my palace. Danaë nodded. I invited the Cyclopes, too, but they said they'd rather go back to bed. Personally, I thought they couldn't wait to get away from the shrieking Perseus.

The Cyclopes quickly packed up their tools and we all made our way out of the cave. I gave Uncle Shiner the emerald and asked him to make a necklace for Persephone. Then my uncles headed for the Cyclopes village while I helped Danaë and Perseus into my chariot. For once Cerberus hopped willingly into the backseat, keeping his distance from the wailing baby.

When we arrived at Villa Pluto, Cerbie ran into the palace and disappeared into some hiding spot. I led Danaë and Perseus into the kitchen. Danaë sat down at the table, holding her son on her lap. It was very late, and all my serving ghosts were asleep, so I started going through the cupboards, searching for something a mortal could eat. It wouldn't do to give them any ambrosia or nectar, the food and drink of the gods. At last, way in the back, I found a box of plain old cheese crackers.

"The sibyl told my father that he would never have a son," Danaë said, picking up where she'd left off. "But she said that he would someday have a grandson who would kill him."

"Uh-oh," I said. Trying to find out the future hardly ever works out. My own dad, Cronus, had gone to see a seer. He was the Ruler of the Universe and the seer told him that his children would dethrone him. Dad was, like, "NO WAY!" So as soon as we kids were born, he swallowed us whole. But then Dad got sick and urped us up, and we fought him and took over. So what the seer said turned out to be true. It always seemed to work that way.

Perseus fought his way out of his mother's arms and slid onto the floor. He crawled into the pantry and began banging on cooking pots.

"He can't hurt anything in there," I said, putting a plate of cheese crackers down in front of her. "Please go on with your story."

"Sad to say, my father has never been fond of me," Danaë said. "He would have killed me to keep the sibyl's prophecy from coming true. But he knows that the gods mete out horrible punishments to mortals who slay their own children, so he decided not to risk it."

"Sounds like quite a guy," I muttered, helping myself to a cracker. Blech! How could mortals stand such tasteless, ambrosia-less snacks?

"My father was determined to keep the prophecy from coming true," Danaë went on. "So he had the brass cage built and sunk deep into the earth. He had me put inside. There is a grate at ground level that allows in sunlight. And servants can pass in food and drink. The only door is guarded by seven fierce dogs, so escape is impossible." Danaë shrugged. "By keeping me prisoner, my father thought to keep me from marrying and bearing a son."

"A cruel plan," I said, feeling almost hungry enough to take another cracker. "And a failure."

"My mother, Queen Aganippe, used to come to me at night, after my father had fallen asleep," Danaë said. "But after a while, she stopped coming.

A servant told me that my father had caught her sneaking out of the palace. That her life was in danger if she ever tried it again. So I was very much alone. Then one evening a shower of golden raindrops fell through the grate of my prison. It was like liquid sunshine. And not so long after that, I gave birth to my son."

"Golden raindrops . . ." I muttered. It sounded familiar.

"I keep Perseus quiet so he will not be discovered," Danaë said. "It is not so easy."

"I'll bet," I said. That baby was a champion wailer.

"If my father discovers Perseus, he will surely find a way to have him killed," Danaë said. "So when he cries, I scream over his cries. The servants think me mad." She shrugged. "It is a small price to pay to keep Perseus safe."

I realized I hadn't heard any banging for a while. "Where is Perseus, anyway?"

Danaë sprang up and rushed into the pantry. Perseus wasn't there. I followed after her as she ran down the palace hallway, calling his name. We looked in the library, the billiard room, the trophy room, the guest ghost room. No Perseus. I stuck my head into the den. My remote lay on the floor with wires and springs sticking out of it. Clearly Perseus had been there. But he wasn't there now. I kept running down the hall until I came to the throne room. The door was ajar. I entered the room, which was empty except for a pair of golden thrones.

"I found him, Danaë!" I called.

Somehow, Perseus had managed to climb up onto my throne. There he sat, kicking his legs and babbling happily. In his chubby little hands he held my crown.

"Perseus!" exclaimed Danaë. "Give me the crown. Come on, give it to Mommy."

With a shriek, the baby hurled the crown to the floor. It rolled under Persephone's throne.

"Don't worry," I told Danaë as I picked it up, and tried to straighten out the bent part. "I hardly ever wear it."

But now I put it on my head and stared at that unruly baby. At his curly black hair, his wide face, his stubborn little mouth. And then it hit me.

I lifted Perseus out of my throne. Over his wails I yelled, "Danaë, that golden rain shower was Zeus, in disguise. He is the father of your child!!!" I handed the baby to his mother.

Danaë looked at me blankly.

"I know it sounds crazy," I told her. "But among us gods, Zeus is famous for taking different forms and fathering as many children as he can. Some of his kids turn out to be immortals, others are mortals. He wants to create a great big Zeus dynasty."

Danaë shook her head. "It is hard to believe, Lord Hades," she said at last. "But it makes as much sense as anything." She looked thoughtfully at her howling son. "You know, I don't think I'll tell Perseus who his father is. It might go to his head."

I nodded. If Perseus was like his father, just about anything would go to his head.

I offered to let Danaë and Perseus stay at Villa Pluto that night, but I was secretly relieved when Danaë shook her head. She was worried for her mother's safety if her father should find her gone. She insisted on returning to the brass box.

"But now I have a doorway," she said, as I helped

her and her shrieking baby back into my chariot. "Now I can take Perseus for outings. And I know the way to Villa Pluto." She smiled. "May we visit you again, Lord Hades?"

Perseus chose that instant to grab my lunx from my girdle. He hurled it to the ground.

"Oh, dear!" said Danaë.

"Don't worry, it's an old lunx," I told Danaë as I bent down to pick up the scattered pieces. "And do come back and visit me any time."

Little did I know then that what I was in for was a whole lot worse than a broken lunx.

Chapter VI

GRRRRR-ILLED

The next weekend, I drove up to see Persephone. When I knocked at her apartment door, she flung it open.

"Hades!" she said. "I've missed you!" She picked up a picnic basket, took my arm, and whisked me outside. We began walking out of the city toward our favorite picnic spot in the countryside. "See the leaf buds on the trees?" Persephone pointed. "And the green shoots poking up out of the earth? I did that."

"Wow, P-phone," I said. "You've really gotten into the whole goddess-of-spring thing."

"That's nothing," said Persephone as we came to a barren field. There wasn't a single bud or blade of grass. "Watch this." She flung her arms wide and shouted, "KA-BLOOM!" As the words left her mouth, clover, buttercups, and violets sprang forth from the earth. Leafless trees sprouted fat pink blossoms. I was impressed.

We spread a cloth in the flowery field and sat down to a picnic, just as we had done the day I fell in love with her—with a little help from Cupid. Persephone took some goodies out of her basket.

"Pickle?" she said, offering me one. "Ambrosia dill. So, Hades, what have you been up to?"

"Plenty," I said. I told her about Athena gorgonizing Medusa and her sisters. I'd had Eno's film developed, and now I pulled out the picture that Athena had snapped. "This was taken just before Athena put the stonifying spell on Medusa." I handed it to Persephone.

"Aaaaahhh!" Persephone cried as she looked at the monsters. "Oh, the poor goddesses! All their gorgeous hair, gone!"

"Well, not gone exactly," I pointed out. "Just

turned to snakes. But at least the Gorgons are in SNIPP now, safe from Athena."

"There is something seriously wrong with Athena, Hades," Persephone said, munching on an ambrosia-laced spring roll. "You know, last summer, Po threw a beach party. All the gods and goddesses went swimming and surfing and had the best time, except for Athena. She showed up wearing her armor! I talked her into taking that off, and Hestia lent her a swimsuit. But Athena refused to take off her helmet. It was so strange. She just sat there on the beach with that helmet on her head, looking miserable."

"Was Medusa at this party?" I asked.

Persephone nodded. "All the moon goddesses came. Medusa set up a water slide and everybody went down it about a million times. We had so much fun."

"Did Medusa and Athena get into a quarrel or anything?" I asked.

Persephone shook her head. "No. Nobody quarreled."

I shrugged. Athena's hatred for Medusa was still a mystery.

Next, I told Persephone about discovering Danaë and Perseus inside their brass prison.

"I can't believe it," Persephone said. "In one week, I've missed so much excitement! Is there anything *else*?"

I gave Persephone her emerald necklace then. It was a hit.

The Underworld Mall was under construction that spring. Dozens of new shops and restaurants were going up. Then my carpenter ghosts went on strike, and I was so busy dealing with labor problems that time passed swiftly. Before long spring had turned to summer, summer became fall, and finally winter rolled around. On December XXI, Cerbie and I drove up to chilly, gray-skied earth to pick up Persephone.

"Those can't *all* be yours!" I exclaimed when I saw P-phone standing outside her apartment beside a mountain of suitcases, trunks, and duffels.

"They are, Hades," Persephone said. "You know it's impossible to shop at the Underworld Mall now. I have six new robes for you. And wait until you see the elegant little throw pillows I bought for the couch! And a set of spun-gold dinner plates. They cost a fortune, but they're worth it."

"I can hardly wait," I said as I began loading her gear. I had to *ZIP!* into Athens to buy a few pack mules, but we finally got all the luggage loaded up. Persephone hopped into the chariot beside me. She was in such a good mood, she even let Cerbie sit in the front seat. Off we drove to the Underworld.

As we carried the suitcases and things into Villa Pluto, Persephone spotted an envelope on the entryway table. It was addressed to both of us.

"What's this? There's no postmark." She opened the envelope. "Listen, Hades.

> *"Dear H and P,*
> *E and R are still you-know-where in the you-know-what, but I had things to do, so I took off.*
> *I'm learning so much! I'll be in touch.*
>
> *—Guess Who"*

Persephone looked puzzled. "Who could this be from?"

I stared at the letter. "Medusa," I said. "My guess is that it means Eno and Riley are still in SNIPP, but that Medusa's left the program."

Persephone nodded. "Medusa is an independent goddess. She must hate hiding out."

"But Athena is out to give her a monstrous tail!" I said.

I reread the letter. *I'm learning so much,* it said. Learning what? I couldn't guess.

Persephone wanted to meet Danaë, so the next night, I asked her and Perseus to come to dinner. I made sure the doors to the throne room were shut tight, then I sent my first lieutenant, Hypnos, the god of sleep, to pick them up.

"You'll like Danaë," I told Persephone as we walked to the entryway to greet our guests. "But I'm not so sure about Perseus."

Hearing the name Perseus, Cerberus turned around and ran off. He wasn't taking any chances.

Danaë and Perseus had never come to visit me. So I hadn't seen them since I'd rescued them from the brass box. When they arrived, I was surprised to see how much Perseus had grown. He was walking now. And he looked more like his father than ever.

"Perseus, can you say hello to Lord Hades and Queen Persephone?" Danaë asked her son.

"NO!" yelled Perseus.

"Oh, come on, Perseus," said Danaë. "You can do it."

"I can do it!" cried Perseus. He broke away from his mother's grasp and ran into the living room, yelling, "I can do it! I can do it!"

"He's such a rascal," said Danaë as she ran after him. She scooped him up and sat down with him on her lap.

Persephone sat down across from her. She and Danaë began talking as if they'd known each other for years. After a few minutes, Persephone turned to me. "Hades, Danaë isn't up on the latest fashions. I want to show her some of the robes and tunics I picked up in Athens. Look after Perseus for a minute, will you?"

"Me?" I said. But Persephone and Danaë were already hurrying from the room.

I turned and saw Perseus over by the couch throwing all the pillows on the floor.

"No, Perseus," I said. "Not Persephone's new pillows!"

He began shrieking and jumping on the pillows.

"No, no!" I told him, trying to pull him off.

Perseus yanked away. "I can do it!" he yelled. "I can do it!"

I quickly picked him up. I knew he'd set up a horrible wail, so—I'm not proud of this—I did the only thing I could think of to keep him from screaming his head off.

"Perseus!" I said. "Let's go find Cerberus. Let's find the doggie."

"Doggie!" Perseus said eagerly. "Doggie!"

"Where is Cerberus?" I said, carrying the boy out of the living room and down the hall. "Is the doggie in here?" I asked, opening a closet door. "Nooooo." I went on down the hall. "Is the doggie in here?" I asked, opening another door. "Nooooo."

"Doggie!" shrieked Perseus. "Want doggie!"

I was sure Cerbie had hidden himself safely away. I was only trying to buy time until Persephone and Danaë had finished their fashion show.

"Is the doggie in here?" I asked, opening the door to a robe closet.

Unfortunately, Cerbie *was* there, hunkered down on the closet floor.

"Doggie!" shrieked Perseus. He kicked me in the stomach and wriggled free. Then he grabbed Cerberus by his stumpy tail and tried to drag him from the closet.

"Let go, Perseus!" I cried.

"I can do it!" yelled Perseus.

"Ow! *Ow!* OW!" howled Cerberus.

Danaë and Persephone heard the commotion and came running.

"Perseus, are you being kind to the nice doggie?" said Danaë.

"Want doggie!" wailed Perseus, keeping his death grip on Cerbie's tail.

"Perseus," said Persephone, "would you like a lollipop?"

"Lolly!" Perseus cried. He let go of the dog.

Persephone took his hand. "Let's go see if we can find one."

My P-phone never failed to amaze me. How clever she was!

I bent down and began what I knew would be a long and humiliating apology to my poor pooch. After much begging, Cerbie came out of the closet. I made an ice pack for him to sit on to soothe his sore tail. I gave him dozens of Cheese Yummies. By bedtime, we were friends again.

Persephone and Danaë became great friends too. That winter, dinner together at Villa Pluto became a weekly event. One night, I paid Meg and Alec handsomely to look after Perseus. But he managed to rip the leather strips from Meg's favorite scourge, the little whip Furies use for punishing mortals. After that, no matter how much I offered to pay, they refused to sit for him.

Danaë knew Perseus was what she called "a busy boy," and when Persephone went back to earth in the spring, she didn't bring him to the palace at all. But the following winter, they became regulars at the dinner table again. Perseus continued to be a stubborn little troublemaker. But Persephone and I liked Danaë's company so much that we were willing to put up with him.

The night before Persephone had to go back to

earth again, Danaë and Perseus came to supper. After we ate, Danaë asked to speak to us. For once, Perseus was sitting under the table, quietly behaving himself.

"Lord Hades and Queen Persephone," Danaë began, "I have been looking for a way to thank you for your great kindness to me and my son. I believe I have found one."

"There's no need to do anything," said Persephone.

"I wish to honor you," said Danaë. "I would like you to be Perseus's god-parents."

"God-parents?" Persephone and I said at the same time. We gods have parents. But we don't have anything called "god-parents." Neither of us understood what she was talking about.

"As Perseus's god-parents," Danaë explained, "you would be there for him. You would watch out for him if he ever needed you. Will you accept this honor?"

Persephone and I were fond of Danaë. We didn't want to hurt her feelings. So we both nodded and said we'd be happy to be Perseus's god-parents.

"We should have some sort of a ceremony,"

Danaë said. "I have heard that the waters of the River Styx are used for important occasions, so this afternoon I walked down to the river and scooped up some of its waters." She pulled a clay pot from her bag and set it on the table.

I didn't like where this whole thing was going.

Danaë bent down to pick up her son. He did not want to be picked up, so he grabbed on to the tablecloth. He gave a yank, and everything on the table, including Persephone's new spun-gold dinner plates, went crashing to the floor.

"Oh, dear," said Danaë.

"Don't worry," I told her. "Persephone never liked those plates anyway."

"Couldn't stand them," agreed my queen.

Danaë picked up the clay pot, which still had a little of the Styx water in it. She held Perseus's hands on it.

"Hades and Persephone, will you also put your hands on this pot?" said Danaë. "Will you now promise to watch over and protect my son, Perseus, come what may?"

Neither Persephone nor I could think of a good

reason why we could not swear this awful oath. And so we put our hands on the pot—alongside the grubby little mitts of Perseus—and swore to protect him, come what may.

I had a bad feeling the whole time I was swearing. Did Danaë know that an oath sworn on the River Styx could never be broken? What had I gotten myself into?

Chapter VII

THE BIG CHEESE

The next morning at dawn, Persephone and I were leaving Villa Pluto when someone slipped a note under the door. I ran to the door and flung it open. No one was there. Only the whiff of ghost.

"What is it, Hades?" asked Persephone. "What does it say?"

I stared at the note. "It's from Medusa!" I exclaimed. We hadn't heard from her in over a year, and I'd been worried. I read it out loud:

"Greetings!

Persephone, when you come back to earth today,
will you bring a small bunch of Stygian riverwort?
I'll send someone to your apartment to pick it up.
You're a peach!

My best to you, Hades!

—Guess Who"

I scratched my head. "What in the Underworld can Medusa want with Stygian riverwort?" The stuff grows like a weed on the banks of the Styx. That's the only place it grows.

"Beats me," said Persephone. "But it's easy enough to get."

I drove Persephone to the river and waited while she picked some wort. Then we went up to earth. When we reached her apartment, I carried in her mountains of luggage. We said our good-byes. Then I drove swiftly back to my kingdom, where I had yet another problem to solve.

Lately, the ghosts had been complaining about

Hermes. They said he was charging their relatives outrageous prices for driving them down to the Underworld on that rickety old bus of his. Being the god of business executives and thieves, Hermes always drives a hard bargain. But now things were getting out of hand.

I waited on the bank of the Styx that morning for Hermes. The little god may have been a thief, but he was punctual. His One-Way to the Underworld bus always arrived at XI o'clock on the dot. But that morning, XI came and went, and no bus arrived. XII, and still no bus. At quarter to I o'clock, I was boiling mad.

"Charon!" I called. "Has Hermes ever been this late before?"

"Never," Charon said. "Usually shows up right on time. I hope nothing's gone wrong," he added. "A poor ferryman can't make a living without any passengers, Lord Hades."

"Spare me, Charon," I muttered. The old river-taxi driver charged each ghost one gold coin to cross the River Styx. If a relative forgot to put a gold coin under a loved one's tongue, that ghost would have to wait on the far shore forever! Charon never, *ever* brought anyone over for free.

I sat down on a rock. My stomach growled. I wished I'd thought to bring a snack. At last I heard a rumble that wasn't my stomach, and I saw the nose of Hermes's ancient bus rounding the last curve of the bumpy Underworld Highway. With a squealing of brakes, the bus came to a stop beside the river. Hermes jumped out.

"Last stop!" Hermes called. He flapped the little wings on his helmet and sandals, and flitted over the heads of the ghosts. "The only stop, actually. Every ghost out!"

I strode over to Hermes. "Where have you been? You're almost two hours late."

"Not my fault!" Hermes flapped higher, just out of my reach. "There was a crowd—"

"Don't try to blame it on traffic," I cut in. "The two of us are the only ones who ever drive on the Underworld Highway!"

"I don't mean traffic," Hermes said, still treading air just above my head. "You know how I pick up my passengers at Ghost Point?" I nodded.

"Well, when I pulled up this morning, a huge crowd was gathered there. All my passengers wandered over to see what was going on, and I couldn't get them rounded up and onto the bus." Hermes fluttered over to some straying ghosts. "Stay in line for the river taxi!" he shouted.

"Will you land, Hermes?" I asked when he flapped back. "I'm getting a stiff neck from trying to look at you."

Hermes fluttered to the ground and sat down on a rock. I sat down, too.

"The King of Argos was there," he said. "He was in a terrible fury."

"King Acrisius?" I said.

Hermes nodded. "His servants dragged a wooden chest to the seashore and the king ordered them to put his daughter inside the chest."

"What?" I shouted, leaping to my feet. "Do you mean Danaë?"

Hermes shrugged. "I don't know her name," he said. "Or the name of her son, who was screaming his head off. At last a servant managed to force him into the chest with his mother."

"Oh, no!" I cried.

"The queen was wailing up a storm," Hermes went on. "She begged the king to let them out of the chest. All the people on shore were crying. Even my passengers were crying, which is unusual for ghosts."

"Hermes! Quick! Tell me what happened!"

"Take it easy, Hades," said Hermes. "The servants nailed the lid onto the chest. Then they carried the chest through the surf to a small boat. The king ordered them to row out beyond the waves, and dump the chest into the sea."

"Did they do this awful deed?" I asked.

Hermes nodded. "So you see, I couldn't very well yank my passengers away—"

I didn't wait to hear any more. I took off running. Minutes later, I was in my chariot galloping up the Underworld Highway. I tried phoning Po as I headed to earth, but he didn't answer. I had to find him. He was my only hope of saving Danaë and Perseus.

I parked at Phaeton's and astro-traveled to Po's island.

"Po!" I cried, running up the walk to Cabana Calypso. "PO!"

A sleepy Po appeared on a palace balcony. "It's the crack of afternoon, Hades."

"It's an emergency, Po!" I called. "You've got to hitch up your dolphins. Now!"

After a few minutes that seemed like hours, Po appeared at the palace door. "You wouldn't believe the party I threw last night—"

"Later, Po," I said, and I told him about Danaë and Perseus.

"Ghost Point?" he said. "Let's go, bro!" We ran down to the dock, and soon we were speeding over the waves. My stomach was lurching with every bump, so I was glad when Po slowed his dolphins. He handed me the reins. "Hold the team steady, Hades. I'll be right back."

"Po!" I cried. "What—"

Po dove into the ocean. I heard a series of clicks, like seashells tapping each other. A minute later, Po rose to the water's surface, and pulled himself into the chariot.

"What were you doing?" I asked him.

"Sending a message to SNIT," Po said. "Coded, of course. If anyone can find that wooden chest, SNIT can. We should be hearing from them any minute now, bro."

Even as Po spoke, two heads popped up out of the water beside Po's chariot.

"Special Agent Corius reporting, Lord Poseidon!" one said in a musical voice.

"Also Special Agent Merius!" said the other.

Both agents wore sea-blue swimming caps monogrammed with the letters SNIT.

"We have spotted the wooden chest," said Special Agent Corius.

"It is barely afloat two nautreds off the island of Seriphos," said Special Agent Merius.

"Seriphos, Seriphos," said Po, thinking. "All right, it's the best we can do. See that it washes safely ashore on the south side of the island. Near the home of Dictys, the fisherman."

"It shall be done, Lord Poseidon!" said Special Agent Corius.

"The south shore," Po repeated. "Not the north shore!"

"Yes, Lord Poseidon!" called Special Agent Merius. "The south shore!" And with that the two disappeared into the sea.

For the first time since I'd heard Hermes's tale, I felt a small flicker of hope.

Po gave a whistle, and his dolphins started off so suddenly that I had to grab on to the side of the chariot to keep from being tossed into the sea.

"We should make Seriphos in ten minutes!" Po shouted to me over the noise of his team. "We'll watch and make sure that Dictys finds the chest and opens it."

"What's wrong with the north shore of Seriphos?" I yelled to Po.

"That's where Dictys's brother, Polydectes, lives," Po yelled back. "Polydectes is the king of the island. He's wicked, Hades. It would be better for Danaë and her son to drown than for them to end up in his hands. Look!" Po shouted, pointing toward a distant shore. "That's Seriphos ahead. And hey, bro, there's the wooden chest!"

I squinted into the distance, searching the sea.

Then I saw it moving at great speed atop the crest of a wave. Agents Corius and Merius had to be under the water, pushing it.

"Next wave, and the thing's beached," said Po.

The trunk rose high on a breaker, which slid it gently up onto the shore.

"Yessss!" Po grinned. "SNIT comes through again."

A mortal who had been fishing in the surf ran over to the trunk. He bent down, inspecting it. He gave a sudden start. Then, with something from his tackle box, he pried off the lid. I held my breath, watching. Slowly, Danaë rose up out of the chest. She held Perseus in her arms. The boy was bawling loudly. Yes! They were alive!

"Wow," said Po. "That boy can really wail."

"Guess who his father is."

"Gotta be Zeus," Po said.

I nodded. "How did you know?"

"No one else could pass on such loud fussing," said Po.

"Well, mission accomplished, Po," I said. "Nice work."

"It was, wasn't it?" Po smiled. "I'll send word to

Dictys and let him know what's what." He revved up his dolphins. "He'll take care of Danaë and Perseus." He turned his chariot around and we headed back to his palace.

"Make sure Dictys doesn't tell anyone who they are," I warned Po. "If King Acrisius finds out that Perseus is alive, he'll send his henchmen to Seriphos to kill him."

"You think they should go into SNIPP?" Po asked.

I shook my head. "Not necessary. Acrisius will never suspect that Danaë and Perseus survived his cruel plot. But what about Polydectes? Does Dictys confide in him?"

"No, Dictys knows what a creep his brother is," Po told me. "Polydectes thinks he's such a big cheese. Way too big to be king of only one little island. I hear he has a scheme to take over all the other islands around here."

"How?" I asked.

"I hate to tell you, bro," said Po. "It's a nasty plot. He's obsessed with having someone bring him Medusa's head."

"Her head?" I couldn't believe what I was hearing!

Po nodded. "He heard what Athena did to Medusa. How anyone who sees her face will be turned to stone. So he's put out the word around here that he'll pay handsomely for anyone who'll go after Medusa, behead her, and bring him her head in a bag."

"That's abominable!" I cried.

"Really," said Po. "I guess he figures he'll row over to another island and ask to see the king. When the king shows up, he'll pull Medusa's head out of the bag. And bingo—the king's a statue."

"He wants to use Medusa's head as a weapon?" I cried. "That makes my ichor boil!"

"Don't worry about Medusa," Po said. "She's in no danger from ol' Poly."

"How do you know?" I said.

"Just trust me on this, bro," said Po.

It took a while for my ichor to simmer down, and we didn't say much for the rest of the trip. When we reached Po's island, I asked him to let me know if there was ever trouble on Seriphos. Then I astro-traveled to my chariot and started for the Underworld. On the way, I thought about Po. He seemed very sure that Medusa was safe. But how could she be? Now she had a vicious goddess *and* an overambitious king trying to slay her. How I wished I could warn her!

When I got home, a letter from Guess Who was waiting for me.

Dear H,
I've put the Stygian riverwort to good use!
I hear you're worried about me. Don't be. I've never been better. E and R are fine, too. E has had some success with her photographs and R is busy sculpting. We think of you often.

—G.W.

I was stunned. The only way Medusa could know I was worried about her was from Po. He must have contacted her right after I left him. Now I *was* worried. If word got out about where Medusa was, Athena would find her for sure. Obviously Po knew where Medusa was hiding. Could I trust my party-animal brother to keep his big mouth shut?

Chapter VIII

CHEESE PUFFERY

Over the years, a few more letters came from Medusa. The latest one said:

> Dear H and P—
> E won a photo contest! R is having a gallery show!
> I'm busy, too. All's well where we are, which is—
> Oops! Can't really say.
>
> —G.W.

She never said much. But Persephone and I were

always grateful to know that she was safe, that Athena hadn't managed to track her down. But we still worried. We didn't understand why Athena hated Medusa and her sisters so much. And until we found out why, there was nothing we could do to turn things around.

Persephone tried her best to find out. Whenever she was on earth or up on Mount Olympus, she made a point of hanging around Athena to see if she could learn anything. And finally one evening, as Cerbie and I were making the rounds of my kingdom, P-phone called me, sounding very excited.

"Hades? I have good news! I had lunch at the Olympus Diner, and guess who was sitting in the next booth? Athena and Hermes! I heard Athena tell Hermes that she'd gone to a seer."

"That's good news?" I asked.

"Just listen, Hades," said Persephone. "Athena asked the seer if she would ever find Medusa. And the seer said she never would, not on her own. That's good news, right?"

"Could be. But with seers, you never know. Is that all the seer said?"

"Well, I couldn't hear everything," Persephone admitted. "And the waiter kept interrupting, trying to tell them the specials, so it was sort of confusing. But I'm pretty sure the seer said Athena could find the Gorgons only with the help of a mortal with a purse. Something like that."

"That could be many mortals," I pointed out.

"It could," agreed Persephone. "Purses are a big accessory right now. But can you picture Athena stooping to ask a mortal for help? I don't think so."

"You're right," I told her. "Maybe this is good news."

We had no sooner said good-bye and hung up, than my phone rang again.

"Big bro? It's me, Po. We have a problem on Seriphos."

"But Po! Just last week you said Dictys was taking good care of Danaë and Perseus."

"He is," said Po. "But Perseus is a handsome young man now."

"Already?" I exclaimed. "Those mortals, they age so fast."

"Perseus is also boastful and obnoxious," Po went on.

"Like father, like son," I said. "But I'm not worried. How much trouble can a boastful young man get into on a little island?"

"Plenty," said Po. "For starters, Danaë is still very beautiful. King Polydectes caught sight of her, and he's been courting her. Now he wants to marry her."

"Danaë doesn't want to marry him, does she?" I asked.

"No way! Danaë can't stand Polydectes," Po said. "Whenever the king comes to visit, Perseus hovers around, protecting her. He brags that he can keep his mother safe from unwelcome suitors. This makes Polydectes furious. He's put the word out that he wouldn't mind if Perseus disappeared. Permanently."

"I'll go to Seriphos now, Po," I said. "I'll talk some sense into Perseus."

At the sound of the name, Cerberus let out a low growl.

"You do that, big bro," said Po. "And, hey, stop by the palace after. I'm having a few minor sea goddesses over for some surf 'n' turf."

"Thanks anyway, Po," I told him. I hung up and turned to my dog. "So, Cerbie, want to come with me to see Perseus?"

Cerberus gave me a triple dirty look, jumped from the chariot, and took off running for Villa Pluto.

I grabbed my helmet from the backseat of the chariot and tossed it into my wallet. Then I turned my steeds toward the well-worn path of the Underworld Highway and drove up to earth. From Phaeton's, I astro-traveled to the north shore of Seriphos, landing next to Polydectes's palace. It was blazing with lights and filled with laughing, talking, tipsy mortals. The king was having a party! I put on my helmet and slipped invisibly into the palace.

I found myself in a huge ballroom. A banner on one wall read CONGRATULATIONS, KING POLYDECTES! Against the opposite wall was a long buffet table. I made my way over to it. Mmmm. Polydectes might be a cruel tyrant, but he sure laid out a nice buffet. I was careful to let no one see the cheese puffs, mini-pizzas, and cheddar crackers floating up off the platters and into my mouth. Yum!

Not bad for an ambrosia–less snack. As I ate, I looked around.

I spotted my host lounging on a golden couch. He wore a golden robe. His thin brown hair was combed over his shiny scalp. He had a skimpy beard and small, cruel eyes. A servant was popping grapes into his mouth.

"Enough grapes," the king snapped. "King Poly want a cracker!"

I ducked out of the way as the servant rushed over to the buffet table.

At the far side of the room, I caught sight of Perseus standing in the midst of a group of young men. I tossed several cheese puffs into my mouth and made my way over to him. Po was right. Perseus had grown into a handsome young man. Yet he was clearly Zeus's son. He had the same curly dark hair, the same stubborn mouth. I would have known him in an instant, even if he hadn't been standing there, boasting and bragging and lying like a pro.

"I caught so many fish today," Perseus was saying. "I bet I set a new world record."

How like his father he sounded!

"Fifty fisherman tried to pull in the net," Perseus went on. "But they couldn't, so I did it, all by myself."

It was clear that Perseus had inherited a good dose of Zeus's myth-o-mania.

Several young men muttered and wandered off. Danaë had never really managed to teach Perseus any social skills. I was about to tap him on the shoulder and tell him I wanted to speak to him, when one of Polydectes's servants climbed up onto a little stagelike platform.

"Attention!" he called. "Presenting King Polydectes and his future bride!"

Bride? I froze. Was Danaë here? Had she agreed to marry this evil king after all?

The guests began to cheer as King Polydectes and a chubby young woman walked up onto the platform. She didn't exactly look overjoyed about being engaged to the king.

"King Polydectes," the servant said. "Your loyal subjects wish you happiness in your marriage to Princess Halia!"

"Here, here!" cried all the guests.

What a relief. Po had gotten it wrong. The king didn't want to marry Danaë after all!

"It is a good thing that Polydectes is marrying Princess Halia," Perseus said to the few young men still gathered around him. "Now he will leave my mother alone."

"Don't bet on it," said the young man standing next to him. "Polydectes is just waiting to see what gifts we're going to give him."

"If our presents aren't good enough, Polydectes won't go through with the wedding," said yet another young man. "He's done it six times before."

"Loyal subjects!" the servant was saying. "You may now reveal the wedding gifts you shall bestow upon the king and his bride!"

Showing gifts before the wedding? I'd never heard of such a custom. If it was common, surely my own bride, Persephone, who knew all about big, splashy weddings, would have told me about it. I drifted back across the ballroom to the buffet table. All the mortals were showing their gifts, so I pretty much had the whole spread to myself. I sampled a cream cheese–stuffed olive. Excellent! I helped myself to several more.

"My king!" one guest called out. "To celebrate your marriage, I shall give you this platter painted with the image of a bull!"

"If you must." King Polydectes sighed. Clearly, a bull platter had not been on his wish list.

"King Polydectes!" another guest called. "I shall give you two silver wine goblets!"

"Only two?" The king yawned, showing a mouthful of half-masticated crackers.

I moved down the table. The figs stuffed with goat cheese looked promising. I took one.

"My king!" called yet another guest. "I shall give you this handsome cheese maker!"

King Polydectes rolled his eyes.

I finished off the figs and moved back to the cheese puffs. They were lighter than air. Yum!

"Your Highness, look! It is a great big cheese maker!" the guest added, realizing that his gift had not been well received. "For making vast quantities of cheese!"

I'd just picked up three more puffs when the

king leaned over and whispered something to his nearest servant.

The servant looked sheepishly into the crowd. "King Polydectes is not satisfied with your gifts," he said. "Do better next week, or his wedding to Princess Halia will be called off."

Princess Halia broke into a grin.

I glanced at Perseus. His fists were clenched. Suddenly, he cried out, "King Polydectes!"

My cheese-puff-filled hand froze halfway to my mouth. What was he up to?

The king looked scornfully down at Perseus.

"Marry Princess Halia!" Perseus cried. "And I shall give you a wondrous gift!"

I stuffed the puffs into my mouth. I hardly tasted them. What was Perseus doing?

King Polydectes sneered. "I'll be the judge of that."

"Marry Halia!" cried Perseus. "And I shall give you what you want most in the world!"

Oh, no, now I knew what he was up to. I had to stop him! I gulped down the puffs and ran toward Perseus. I'd grab him and—*POOF!*—he'd vanish into thin air. Then I'd figure out what to do with him.

"Name it," growled the king. "Or be still."

And before I could get to him, the foolish young man cried out, "I, Perseus, swear to bring you the head of the Gorgon Medusa!"

I nearly choked on my cheese puffs.

I was too late!

Chapter IX

SMOKED, BUT GOUDA

A smile spread slowly across Polydectes's thin lips. A smile that told me Perseus had fallen into the evil king's trap!

Polydectes wanted to be rid of the boy. If Perseus found Medusa and looked at her, he'd be turned to stone. That was the *real* present the king was hoping for. Then King Polydectes would be free to marry Danaë. But, if Perseus somehow managed to bring the king Medusa's head? Then Polydectes would have his dream weapon. It was a win-win game for old Poly-D.

"Yes," Polydectes told Perseus. "This is what I most desire. But tell me, boy. How will you find Medusa? No one knows where she lives."

"I shall go to the oracle at Delphi!" Perseus declared.

I winced. Where had he gotten this brilliant idea—from his grandfather, King Acrisius?

"The sibyl will tell me where to find the Gorgons," Perseus went on. "I shall travel to their hideaway, however far it may be. And I, Perseus, will cut off Medusa's head and bring it to you!"

My ichor started boiling all over again. These mortals! They were shameless.

"Go, then," said Polydectes. "And do as you have sworn."

Perseus turned and walked quickly out of the ballroom. I circled by the buffet, scooped up one last handful of cheese puffs, then followed Perseus into the night.

Perseus headed down to the beach and began untying a rowboat. The last thing I wanted to do was take a boat ride. I thought about astro-traveling to Delphi and meeting Perseus there when he arrived. But as I watched him struggling with the rope, I realized that he needed my help—even to get his boat untied! So I lent my invisible fingers to the task, then leaped from the shore into the boat.

"Ye gods!" exclaimed Perseus as I landed with an invisible thud. "What strange winds blow this night?" He steadied the little craft and began rowing away from Seriphos. The waves were high and Perseus was a lousy oarsman. With all those cheese puffs sloshing around in my gut, it took all my godly willpower not to get seasick.

"I can do it!" Perseus mumbled to himself as he rowed. "I will bring Polydectes the Gorgon's head. Then he will marry Halia and leave my mother alone. I can do it!"

This, from a mortal without a sword. Without a helmet. Without a plan. Only a son of Zeus could have so much misplaced confidence.

Perseus rowed on. Finally, I spotted the shore of Greece, and not a moment too soon. If I hadn't been invisible, I would have been a sickly shade of green.

Perseus pulled the boat ashore and started walking north toward Delphi. I trudged along beside him. After a while, my feet began to hurt, and I was reminded of the old days, when the only way we gods could get anywhere was to walk, run, or jog. We even had to hike up Mount Olympus to get home. Then we learned how to astro-travel, and that was the end of blisters on our godly feet. Sometimes I think it's the little things like astro-traveling that make being a god so worthwhile.

It took three days for Perseus and me to hike to Delphi. When we arrived, we looked up at the oracle's temple, which sat halfway up Mount Parnassus, on its steepest side. A sulphurous yellow haze hung over the mountain. No birds sang in the trees. No nymphs frolicked in the nearby streams. It was a place of smoke and silence.

Perseus started up the stone steps cut into the mountain. I was right behind him. The path was lined with signs for the Mount Parnassus Hotel, which advertised, among other luxuries, a smoke-warmed hot tub and shuttle service direct to the sibyl. There were souvenir stands, too. One featured THE ONE AND ONLY TALKING SIBYL DOLL! PRESS THE BUTTON AND SHE'LL TELL YOU THE FUTURE!

Perseus stepped up to the first official-looking mortal he saw—a woman wearing a badge that read HI! MY NAME'S VALIA! WELCOME TO DELPHI!

"I am here to see the sibyl," Perseus announced.

"You and half of Greece," muttered Valia. "There's the line."

Perseus looked where Valia pointed. The line wound all the way around the base of the mountain. "Ye gods!" said Perseus. "Is there no way I can cut to the front of this line?"

"Could be," Valia said. "What have you got, gold coins?"

"I have no gold," said Perseus.

"Silver?" said Valia.

"I have no silver," said Perseus.

"Probably no jewels, either, huh?" said Valia.

Perseus shook his head.

Valia shrugged. "As I said, there's the line."

Perseus walked over to the end of the line. I figured it would be a good three-hour wait. That gave me a chance to carry out a little scheme of my own.

I left Perseus standing in line and continued

invisibly up the path until I reached the oracle entrance. Taking care not to bump into any of the waiting mortals, I flipped the OPEN sign over so that it read CLOSED. Then I slipped into the cave. The sibyl, a young mortal priestess, sat on a tripod—a high three-legged stool—on the very edge of an enormous crack in the cave floor. Clouds of yellow smoke rose up from some mysterious source below.

"Pssst!" I said. "Sibyl?"

The sibyl turned her head, looking around. Her eyes were very bloodshot. And no wonder—all that smoke could not have been good for her.

"It's me, Hades, King of the Underworld," I said. "I'm here, but I'm invisible."

The sibyl closed her eyes. "Speak, pilgrim! What is your question for the oracle?"

"I'm not a pilgrim myself," I explained. "But I'm here with one. His name is Perseus. He's going to ask you where to find Medusa the Gorgon."

The sibyl frowned. "Go on."

"Could you do me a huge favor, Sibyl?" I said. "Could you tell Perseus that Medusa lives in the opposite direction from where she really lives?"

The sibyl's eyes popped open in surprise.

Suddenly the ground began to rumble.

WHOOSH! An angry billow of dark gray smoke belched up from the crevice. It was so thick I lost sight of the sibyl. I could hardly breathe.

"HADES, IS THAT YOU?" a voice called from inside the smoke.

"Uh, yeah," I managed.

"IT'S ME, MOTHER EARTH," said the voice. "YOUR GRANNY GAIA."

"Granny!" I said. "This is a surprise."

"WHY?" snapped Granny Gaia. "WHO DID YOU THINK WOULD BE SPEAKING TO YOU FROM DEEP INSIDE THE EARTH, A WOOD SPRITE? NOW, LISTEN HERE, HADES. DID I JUST HEAR YOU ASK MY SIBYL TO FIB?"

"I—I guess you could say that," I admitted, coughing from the smoke. "But it's for a worthy cause, Granny. Perseus wants to find Medusa so he can behead her!"

"IF THAT IS HER FATE, SO BE IT," snapped Granny Gaia. "I HAVE MY REPUTATION TO MAINTAIN HERE, HADES. IF MY SIBYL

STARTED LYING AND STRETCHING THE
TRUTH WHENEVER IT SUITED ONE OF
YOU GODS, NO ONE WOULD TRUST THIS
ORACLE. NO ONE WOULD PAY TO SEE THE
SIBYL. I HAVE MY RETIREMENT TO
CONSIDER!"

"I see your point, but—"

"GOOD." Granny Gaia cut me off.

"But Granny!" I cried. "Poor Medusa! She's—"

"GO AWAY, HADES," said Granny Gaia. "AND
DON'T MEDDLE WITH MY SIBYL."

There was another *WHOOSH!* The gray smoke
was sucked back into the crevice. Once more,
sulphurous yellow smoke floated up to take its place.

"Next pilgrim!" called the sibyl.

I made my invisible way out of the cave and
flipped the sign back to OPEN. I couldn't believe it.
Foiled by my own granny!

Perseus stood next in line. I should have known
he'd find a way to cut ahead. He was talking to an
oracle official whose name tag read LELIX.

"That will be LX drachmas," said Lelix.

"There's a charge?" asked Perseus.

Lelix glared at him. "Take a look up there." He pointed to a huge serpent that was coiled around the top of Mount Parnassus. "That's Python. He's the guard here. And he makes sure no one gets in to see the sibyl for free."

"How about an IOU?" asked Perseus. He and Lelix haggled for a while. Finally Perseus signed a slip of parchment. If Perseus was anything like his father, Lelix was going to have that IOU forever. When the deal was done, I followed Perseus back into the cave.

The sibyl gazed at Perseus. "Speak, pilgrim," she said in a low voice. "What is your question for the oracle?"

Perseus said, "Where is the home of Medusa the Gorgon?"

The sibyl leaned forward over the smoky crevice and called down the question: "Where is the home of Medusa the Gorgon?" She leaned so far that two legs of her tripod left the ground. There, she balanced, over the chasm, with her eyes closed and smoke billowing up into her face.

At last the sibyl leaned back, raised her head and

turned slowly toward Perseus. "Mother Earth has spoken. You must go to the Land of the Acorn Eaters!"

I groaned inwardly. I'd been to that land, also known as Dodona. It was filled with thousands of oaks, the tree sacred to Zeus. The oak trees of Dodona had the power of speech, and they babbled incessantly, revealing the will of Zeus.

"Land of the Acorn Eaters?" said Perseus. "Where's that?"

The sibyl sat with her head bowed. She made no answer.

"Wait a minute, that's it?" said Perseus.

The sibyl was silent.

"What kind of answer is that?" cried Perseus. "I came all this way for one sentence?"

The sibyl was as silent as a stone.

"Excuse me, but I'm the next pilgrim," said a mortal coming up behind Perseus. "I think your time's up."

Perseus gave a grunt of frustration and stomped angrily out of the cave.

These mortals, I thought, hurrying after him. They expect so much.

Chapter X

SHARPER CHEDDAR

I stuck with Perseus for four days as he hiked, rowed, sailed, hitched, and climbed his way to Dodona. At last we reached the Land of the Acorn Eaters. There were oak trees everywhere, as far as the eye could see, and the place was totally overrun with squirrels. The inhabitants of Dodona were small, scrawny mortals. They all wore helmets to protect their heads from falling acorns as they darted among the oak trees collecting acorns to make flour for their world-famous Dodona acorn bread. They had to move fast, or the squirrels beat them to the acorns.

Perseus bought a hunk of cheese and a loaf of Dodona bread from a little roadside stand with another IOU. I left him sitting by the side of the road, munching, while I astro-traveled into the town of Dodona to see if I could find some yummier eats. The best I could do was an acorn burger with a side of acorn fries at the local diner. I ate quickly and *ZIPPED!* myself back to where I'd left Perseus. But by the time I got there, he was gone. I couldn't let that pesky mortal out of my sight for two minutes!

I walked invisibly down the road, keeping my ears open. I figured I'd hear about Perseus from the oaks. But they only shouted, "Who's the fairest god of all? Zeus!" and "Tonight on the Zeus Channel: Zeus meets Homer on *The Olympsons!* Don't miss it!" Or they bragged to each other about having the biggest acorns.

I kept going. At last I heard a promising conversation and stopped to listen.

"Of course he's a god," said a tall oak. Moss covered the north side of its trunk.

"No, he's a mortal," said a bushier oak on the other side of the road.

"He looks just like Zeus," said the tall oak. "I say he's a god and I'm bigger, so what I say goes!"

"Oh, you don't know everything!" said the bushy oak.

I winced. They both sounded like Zeus!

"Here he comes again!" said the tall oak. "If he isn't a god, I'll drop my leaves."

"Big deal," said the bushy oak. "You'll drop your leaves anyway, come fall."

I squinted down the road. Sure enough, here came Perseus.

"Which of you oaks can tell me where Medusa dwells?" Perseus was shouting to the trees.

But the oaks only shrugged their branches. I smiled. They didn't have a clue.

When Perseus reached the spot on the road between the tall oak and the bushy oak, he stopped. "Who can tell me where the Gorgons live?" he cried.

"We can only know what Zeus knows," the tall oak told Perseus.

"Zeus knows practically everything," said the bushy oak. "But the one thing he doesn't know is where the Gorgons live."

"But he must!" cried Perseus. "The sibyl at Delphi sent me here to find out. She wouldn't have done that if you couldn't help me."

"Oh, don't be so sure," said the tall oak. "This could be the first stop on a quest."

"And by the way, you're a mortal, aren't you?" asked the bushy oak.

"Yes," said Perseus.

"Ha! I told you so!" said the bushy oak to the tall oak. "Okay, drop your leaves! That was the deal. Oh, you're going to look so funny when you're bald!"

These oaks were Zeus with bark!

The tall oak sighed and started flinging its branches about in a most alarming manner. Squirrels leaped into neighboring trees as leaves began flying in every direction.

"Hey, watch it!" said Perseus, jumping out of the way.

In no time, the tall oak's branches were bare. "Happy now?" he asked the bushy tree.

"You look awful!" said the bushy oak.

"So don't look," said the tall oak. "I'll grow new leaves next spring."

Spring! The very word made me think of Persephone. How I wished I could be done with Perseus so I could go to Athens and visit her.

"I beg you!" Perseus said to the oaks. "Tell me something that will help me find Medusa."

"We can only tell you what Zeus knows," warned the tall oak.

Just then an owl flew down and perched on a bare branch of the tall oak. What was an owl doing, flying around in the daytime? I had a bad feeling about that bird.

"All right," Perseus said to the oaks. "Tell me something Zeus knows."

The oaks bent their trunks so that their branches nearly scraped the earth. Then they rose, and they both began talking at once.

"You are under the protection of the gods!" said the tall oak.

"Hoo!" said the owl.

"You, Perseus," said the bushy oak. "The gods are watching out for you."

How did the oaks know that I was looking out for Perseus? Had Po mentioned it to Zeus?

"Which gods?" asked Perseus. "All of them?"

"Not all," said the bushy oak.

"The gods hardly ever team up that way," said the tall oak.

"They can never agree among themselves," said the bushy oak.

"More likely one or two gods," said the tall oak. "Maybe three, but that's the limit."

"Hoo, hoo!" hooted the owl.

"Me. Protected by the gods." Perseus smiled. "I always knew I was a pretty special mortal. This proves it. But tell me, oaks. How can I call upon these gods to help me find Medusa?"

"Oh, you can't call upon them," said the bushy oak.

"No, they'll call upon you," said the tall oak. "*If* they feel like it."

"That's how it works," said the bushy oak.

"So I just have to wait?" said Perseus. "But I hate waiting."

I stifled a laugh. Like father, like son!

Suddenly a blinding flash lit the sky. It was followed by a second equally blinding flash.

"Yikes!" said Perseus. "What's going on?"

Out of the light Athena and Hermes appeared. I knew that owl was a bad omen!

"Great acorn caps!" exclaimed the tall oak.

Was I ever glad I was invisible. Now it became clear to me that I wasn't the god the oaks meant at all. Perseus was under the protection of *these* two clowns.

"Greetings Perseus!" said Athena and Hermes together.

Most mortals would have been struck speechless by the appearance of two powerful Olympians. But not Perseus. "Greetings, immortals!" he replied.

"I am Athena," said the goddess. "This is Hermes. We were sent by your father, Zeus."

"Ha!" exclaimed the cocky Perseus. "I knew my dad was a bigwig."

"Zeus said to tell you he's sorry you turned out to be a mortal," said Hermes.

"I told you he was a mortal," said the bushy oak. "He had mortal written all over him."

"Oh, drop it, will you?" said the tall oak.

"We have come to aid you in your quest to slay Medusa," Athena told Perseus.

"I don't need any help," Perseus declared. "I can do it myself!"

"No one turns down the help of the gods," said Hermes.

"I do!" said stubborn Perseus. "A hero must act alone."

Athena rolled her eyes at such an attitude. "I have unfinished business with Medusa," she said through clenched teeth. "A seer told me that I can find Medusa only with your help, Perseus. I need you to lead me to her!"

Hearing this, my invisible jaw dropped open. So much for Persephone's theory about Athena needing a *mortal with a purse.* The seer had meant *mortal Perseus*!

"I shall find Medusa and behead her!" cried Perseus. "But I must do it alone."

Athena swallowed. I could tell she would have liked to run her spear through this bullheaded mortal, but she restrained herself.

"All right, Perseus," Athena managed to say. "We won't step in when you do the deed. But at least let us equip you as a hero. Having the right tools for the job can make a huge difference."

"A humongous difference," said Hermes. "Plus, looking your best while doing heroic deeds is essential. You know, for all the hero artwork that comes afterward. The paintings, the statues, and so forth. That's why we ordered you some gear from the Sharper Mortals Catalog. Here, take this." He handed Hermes what looked like a very sharp sickle. "It's the Ultralite Gorgon Scaler Deluxe. This baby can slice through anything."

Perseus clipped the sickle to his girdle. "Thank you, Hermes."

"He has good manners," said the bushy oak.

"For a mortal," said the tall oak.

"And these," Hermes went on, "are winged sandals."

Perseus wrinkled his nose. "They've been *worn*."

"They're vintage!" exclaimed Hermes. "These little booties cost three times what a new pair of winged sandals costs—*if* you can even find a pair in your size!" Hermes stepped back to admire the sandals as Perseus put them on. "No more trudging from land to land on your quest to find out where Medusa lives. Now you can fly!"

Perseus smiled. "How do I get them to flap?"

"There's a little button on the inside ankle strap of each sandal," said Hermes.

"Next item," said Athena. She handed Perseus the shiniest shield I'd ever seen.

"Oh!" exclaimed Perseus, looking happily into the shield. "The eyes! The hair! The chin! Very handsome. Thank you for the mirror."

"It's not just a mirror, Perseus," said Athena patiently. "It's a Mirror-Shield Utility Combination. It comes with a voice mechanism, too. Listen." She pressed a lever on the edge of the shield and a loud voice called out, "*Surrender immediately!*"

"I can shout that out myself," said Perseus.

"The voice mechanism is totally optional," said Athena. "Now, when you find Medusa, you know not to look directly at her, don't you, Perseus?"

"Of course!" said Perseus. "Any idiot knows that."

"Right," said Athena. "But cutting off her head without looking at her might be tricky."

"Not for me," bragged Perseus.

"Even for you," Athena said. "But if you look at her reflection in this shield? No problem."

"You mean I can look at her in the shield and not be turned to stone?" asked Perseus.

"Exactly." Athena smiled. "And Medusa will be history!"

"I am ready!" cried Perseus.

"Not quite," said Hermes. "You need two more items to complete your mission. They aren't available from the Sharper Mortal Catalog. These two you can find only by going—"

I felt a buzzing sensation on my scalp, then a jolt. Suddenly I was visible again! Yikes! I jumped behind the bushy oak.

"Intruder! Interloper!" the tall oak called out.

"Hiding behind me!" called the bushy oak.

"Shhh!" I said, kicking at its trunk.

"Ow!" cried the bushy oak. "He strikes the sacred oaks of Zeus!"

Luckily, the impact of the kick jarred my helmet, and I disappeared again.

Hermes looked around. "I don't see anyone, oaks." He turned back to Perseus. "After you get these two items, go to the foot of Mount Atlas. Athena and I will meet you there tomorrow."

"I'll be there," said Perseus. He bent down and pressed the buttons on his sandals. The wings began flapping, lifting him into the air. "Whoa!" he cried, flailing his arms, lurching forward and backward. In this awkward state, Perseus disappeared into the sky.

I was about to take off after him when my helmet started buzzing. I hated to leave Perseus on his own, but I couldn't take a chance on my helmet shorting out again. The thought of what might happen if Athena saw me made my ichor ice up.

So, instead of tailing Perseus, I quickly astro-traveled back to Phaeton's garage. I whipped off my sputtering helmet and slipped it into my wallet. I'd take it right to the Cyclopes. Uncle Shiner could fix it for me and I'd be back on the trail with Perseus in no time. Off I drove to the Underworld, happy to have left Dodona and its yakking oaks far behind.

Chapter XI

CHEESE YUMMIES

It was after midnight by the time I crossed the River Styx. I galloped straight to the Cyclopes Village, jumped out of my chariot, and ran to the forge. A sign on the door read CLOSED, so I hurried over to my Uncle Shiner's condo and pounded on the door. There was no answer. I knocked on Lightninger's door. And on Thunderer's. Nobody was home. My Cyclopes uncles had a more active social life than I'd realized.

I'd have to wait until the next morning to get my helmet fixed. Who knew what sort of trouble Perseus could get into by then?

I drove to Villa Pluto. When I walked into the den, I found Cerbie asleep on the couch. "Hello, pooch," I said.

At the sound of my voice, the dog lifted his heads but he didn't run to greet me. It seemed his noses were still out of joint because I'd gone off to help Perseus.

Hanging out with Perseus had taken its toll. I was weak from lack of proper godly food. The Furies had just flown home from a night of avenging, so I ordered two extra-ambrosia pizzas and a VI-pack of Necta-Colas from di Minos Pizza and invited them to dine with me. Over pizza, I filled them in on what was going on with Perseus and Medusa.

After we ate, I stood up and stretched. "Time for me to hit the hay, ladies," I said. "I have to get up extra early to see Shiner about my helmet."

"Probably just needs a new battery, Hades," said Tisi. "Come on, sisters. Let's go get our beauty rest, too."

I went to my bedroom, took the Helmet of Darkness out of my wallet, and watched it grow to its full size. I laid it on my dresser next to my wallet.

I brushed my teeth, put on my pajamas, and climbed into bed. A minute later, Cerbie came in and curled up at my feet, and I knew I was forgiven.

I had strange dreams all night long. Cerbie, growling and whining. Shadows, coming and going. When I opened my eyes the next morning, I was exhausted.

Right away, I knew something was wrong. Cerbie wasn't on the bed. And an odd damp smell hung in the air. I sat up and looked around. My helmet! It was gone!

I jumped up. "Cerbie!" I called. "Come!"

But the dog didn't come. I called and called, but Cerbie seemed to be missing, too. I ran into the kitchen. The Furies were having their morning ambrosia java.

"Tisi? Meg? Alec?" I said. "Did you take my helmet over to the Cyclopes to get it fixed?"

"Hades, you know we never run your errands," Tisi said. "What's wrong?"

I sank into a chair. "My dog is gone and my helmet is missing!"

"Let's check your room, Hades," suggested Meg.

"Maybe Cerbie's asleep under the bed. Maybe your helmet rolled onto the floor."

"Maybe," I said, hoping it was true. I ran after them to my room, calling "Cerbie! Cerbie!"

At the doorway, I stopped. I thought I heard the faint sound of three dogs whimpering. The Furies went on into my room, but I continued down the hallway. The whimpering grew louder. I stopped at Persephone's out-of-season sandals closet and threw open the door. Cerbie sprang out.

"Cerbie!" I cried. "Who shut you in there?"

Cerberus sniffed. He threw his shoulders back, put all his heads up, and walked ahead of me back to my room.

"I found Cerbie," I told the Furies. "Someone shut him in a closet!"

"Poor pup, pup, pup!" said Tisi, bending down to give him a pat. "Did we have an intruder, Cerbie?"

Cerbie gave a triple sneeze, and ignored the question.

"Hades!" Meg called. She stood in front of my dresser. "Look, puddles!"

"Is anything besides your helmet missing, Hades?" asked Tisi.

I made a quick survey of the room. "Nothing that I can—" I stared at the top of my dresser. "My wallet!" I cried. "My K.H.R.O.T.U. wallet! It was here, next to my helmet."

"I see footprints," Alec called suddenly. "Wet, webbed footprints."

Tisi had the best nose of the three. She extended her head so that her nose was directly over the footprints and sniffed. "I smell naiad."

"That's the scent," exclaimed Meg. "The Stygian Naiads!"

"I'll fetch them *now*!" cried Alec, and off she raced.

The Stygian Naiads were the water nymphs Athena had zapped with her dog-head spell. Several of them lived in a little pool beside the River Styx, but I hardly ever saw them. They were so ashamed of their looks that they almost never left their pool.

Cerberus began growling, and seconds later, Alec brought in two Naiads. "Naiad Fida and Naiad Rova." She folded her arms across her chest, and added, "They have already confessed."

"You took my helmet and wallet?" I asked them.

"Yes!" cried Fida. Tears streamed down her muzzle. "We're sorry!"

"But why?" I asked.

"We did it for Perseus!" cried Rova. She was crying, too, and drooling up a storm.

"Perseus?" I cried, not wanting to believe my ears. "What's *he* got to do with this?"

"He came to see us at our pool," said Rova.

That sneaky Hermes! He must have told Perseus about the shortcut to the Underworld!

"He told us we were beautiful," said Fida. "He scratched us under our chins."

"He promised to come back, bringing friends for all of us," said Rova. "He said he and his friends would take us dancing up in Athens!"

Fat chance! Ohhh, Perseus was exactly like his scheming myth-o-maniac father.

"But he said all this would happen only if you stole my helmet and my wallet for him?" I asked. "Am I right?"

Fida and Rova nodded, still weeping pitifully.

"We led Perseus here," said Rova. "We tiptoed, very quietly. You were sound asleep."

"What about Cerberus?" I asked. "Why didn't he bark and wake me?"

"We know Cerberus loves Cheese Yummies," said Fida. "We used them to lure Cerberus out of the room. Then, before he could make a racket—"

"Perseus shut him up in the closet," I finished for her.

Fida nodded sorrowfully.

Cerberus was lying by the window, his back end toward us. He pretended not to hear this tale of his seduction by Cheese Yummies.

"Then we stole your helmet and wallet and gave them to Perseus," said Rova.

At least now I knew what the last two items on Athena and Hermes's list were!

"Are you going to punish us?" asked Fida.

"We take care of that end of things," said Alec.

"Did Perseus say where he was going?" I asked the Naiads.

"To Mount Atlas," Rova said. "To see the Gray Sisters."

"Oh, no!" I cried. How did Athena and Hermes know about the Gorgon's older sisters? Then I remembered—Medusa had told everyone in her family about her big sisters. Well, word had spread. I had to beat Perseus to those Gray Sisters!

"You've been very helpful," I told the Naiads. "So we won't punish you. Good-bye!"

"Thank you, King Hades!" said Fida. "We won't betray you again."

"Until the next handsome young mortal invites you out dancing," said Alec.

"Is another one coming?" asked Rova, her eyes lighting up.

"Let's go tell the others!" said Fida.

Alec opened the door, and the Naiads scampered out.

"Alec, that wasn't nice," I said.

"Sorry, Hades," she said. "But it wasn't right that they should go completely unpunished."

"I guess a little hopeful primping won't do them any harm," I said. "Tell me, Furies, do you know where the Gray Sisters live?"

"Of course we do," said Tisi.

"We sometimes stop and have tea with them," said Meg.

"And sandwiches," said Alec.

"Good!" I said. "And now, I have another task for you."

"Just ask, Hades," said Tisi.

"We'll help you!" said Meg.

"Tell us what you want *now*!" said Alec.

"Pack your overnight bags, ladies," I said. "Quickly! I need you to fly me to Mount Atlas."

Chapter XII

CHEESY PERSEUS

"We can't fly you anywhere, Hades," said Tisi.

"You're too . . . uh, too, uh . . ." Meg sputtered.

"Too heavy!" said Alec.

"You'll just have to flap extra hard," I insisted. "Driving up to earth will take too long. I have to get to Mount Atlas on the double. Medusa's life is at stake! And, come to think of it, so is Perseus's."

The Furies hurried into their wing of the palace. When they reappeared, they had their overnight bags, stylish little black leather backpacks that fit snugly between their wings.

"Going like that, Hades?" asked Tisi.

Only then did I realize I still had on my jammies, red flannel with an orange flame pattern. I ran into my bedroom, put on a proper godly robe, and stuffed everything the Naiads hadn't stolen into my pockets. Then I tossed some ambrosia-cheese crackers into a bag. I told Cerbie good-bye, and we all raced out of Villa Pluto.

Meg and Alec bent their knees and gripped each other's forearms to make a seat for me the way they'd once done for Persephone. I sat down.

"Uuugh!" said Meg.

"You weigh a dekaton!" said Alec.

I put my arms around their shoulders. Then— *Thwap! Thwap! Thwap!*—the Furies opened their great black wings and rose off the ground. Well, Tisi rose. Meg and Alec flapped like crazy, but they didn't gain much altitude.

"I'm not sure we can carry you, Hades," Meg gasped.

"You need to lose weight *now!*" said Alec.

Just when it looked as if we were going to run smack into the asphodel hedge, the wind gusted, filling their mighty wings with air. Soon we were soaring through the sky.

"Eagle ahead!" I warned the Furies. "Veer to the right. But don't go through those clouds. We don't want to lose sight of Tisi."

Finally Alec said, "Relax, Hades! *Now!*"

And that put an end to my backseat flying.

It wasn't long before Mount Atlas appeared ahead of us. The Furies circled it until Tisi saw the Gray Sisters' cottage. It sat in the middle of a meadow encircled by craggy rocks.

"Hold on, Hades," said Meg.

"Coming in for a landing," said Alec. *"Now!"*

I closed my eyes and—*THUMP!* We hit the ground. I ran a few steps and came to a stop. The Furies folded their wings. Keeping low, we made our way toward the circle of rocks. If Perseus was already there, we didn't want him to see us.

Slowly we raised our heads and peered over the rocks. I'd expected the Gray Sisters to look something like Eno, Riley, and Medusa before they'd been gorgonized.

Wrong!

The Gray Sisters were three strange birds. Swans, actually. They were perched on the backs of garden chairs, around a small table, having tea. Under their swan's wings, they had slender gray arms and hands, which they used to pass around the teapot. On top of their long swans' necks they had small women's heads. Their long gray hair hid their faces from view.

"Who's who?" I whispered to Tisi.

"Pemphredo has the eye now," Tisi whispered back.

"The eye?" I said.

Tisi nodded. "There's just one eyeball, so the three sisters have to share it."

Now I understood what Medusa meant when she said they had some unfortunate physical characteristics!

"Enyo is next to her," Tisi went on. "And the one with the tooth is Deino."

"Just one tooth, too, eh?" I asked.

Tisi nodded.

Suddenly there was a loud crash.

Pemphredo put down her bread. "What was

that?" she exclaimed, scanning the garden with a big blue eye.

"What do you see, Phreddy?" cried Enyo. "What? What?"

"Nothing yet," said Pemphredo, still looking around.

"Give me the eye!" said Deino. "Let me look!"

"Wait your turn," said Pemphredo firmly. "I just put it in."

The Gray Sisters were quiet, listening. We held still, too. I heard the sound of footsteps. Suddenly, Perseus appeared. His sandal wings flapped like crazy as he fought to stay aloft. The Gorgon Scaler swung back and forth from his girdle. And on his head, my Helmet of Darkness was shorting out and firing off sparks.

I smiled.

Perseus clicked his ankles together, the sandal wings stopped flapping, and he crashed to the ground. He managed to hang onto Athena's big shield with one hand. With the other hand, he yanked the helmet from his head. "Drat this thing!" he muttered as he struggled to his feet.

"Who are you, mortal?" demanded Pemphredo.

"I am Perseus!" my god-son declared.

"Is he handsome?" said Enyo. "Let me see him!"

"It's my turn next!" said Deino. "Phreddy, give me the eye!"

"Oh, all right," said Pemphredo. She gently squeezed her eye socket, and the eyeball popped out. She caught it expertly and held it out in her hand. Deino fumbled for it and at last made contact. She plucked up the eyeball and quickly pressed it into her own socket. She blinked a few times, rolled the eye, and then directed her gaze toward Perseus.

"Oh, he is handsome!" said Deino, opening the eye wide. Now, it was a brown eye. "Why have you come all this way to visit us, handsome Perseus?"

"So that you can tell me where the Gorgons live!" said Perseus.

"Why?" asked Deino. "What do you want with our little sisters?"

"I, uh . . . I want to tell them about the big prize they've won," said Perseus.

"Myth-o-maniac!" I muttered between gritted teeth. "I'm going to put a stop to this!"

Tisi put a hand on my shoulder. "Wait, Hades," she whispered. "I'll bet Hermes and Athena are lurking around here to see how their little hero is doing."

I nodded. "No doubt."

"If you jump in now," Tisi went on, "you'll just get into a big fight with them, and we'll never find out where Medusa lives. Let's wait and hear what the Gray Sisters have to say."

"You're right," I said, squatting back down and peering between the rocks. "But wait until I get my hands on that little liar!"

"The prize is a great big cheese maker," Perseus was saying.

"Oh, Medusa loves cheese," said Pemphredo. "How did our sisters win this prize?"

"They—um—they entered a contest," said Perseus. "They had to write, in five hundred words or less, who in the whole universe they would most like to have lunch with."

How easily the lies rolled off his tongue!

"Can we enter the contest?" asked Pemphredo. "I know who I'd have lunch with—Argus! He has a hundred eyes. I'd try to talk him into giving me one."

"I want one, too!" said Deino.

"I haven't seen Perseus yet," Enyo whined. "Give me the eye, Deino."

"Oh, all right," said Deino. She took a last look at my god-son. Then she squeezed her socket, popped out the eye, and extended her hand to Enyo. But as Enyo groped for her sister's hand, Perseus quickly lunged forward and seized the eyeball.

"Enyo," said Deino. "You don't have to grab!"

"I didn't!" said Enyo. "Where's the eye?"

"You know you took it," said Deino. "Very rudely, I might add."

"I didn't take it," said Enyo. "Phreddy? Did you take it?"

"Not me," said Pemphredo.

"I took it," Perseus declared. "I have your eyeball, and—yuck! Is it ever slimy!"

"Our eyeball!" wailed Enyo. "Our only eyeball! Give it back!"

"Okay," agreed Perseus. "As soon as you tell me where to find the Gorgons."

"This is blackmail!" said Deino.

"Call it what you will," said Perseus. "No address, no eyeball."

"There never was any contest or any cheese maker, was there?" said Pemphredo.

"I was trying to make it easy for you," said Perseus. "But you forced me to play hardball. Hard *eye*ball." Perseus chuckled at his own bad joke.

The three Gray Sisters leaned forward over the table, whispering.

I shook my head. "I should have stopped him when I had the chance."

"Who knew Perseus was *this* cheesy?" said Tisi. "But maybe we can learn something yet."

"You'd better tell me the truth," said Perseus. He dropped the eyeball into the Helmet of Darkness, and wiped his fingers on his robe. "If you don't," he continued, "I'll come back here and play a little game of Stomp on the Eyeball!"

"Not that!" cried Enyo. "We'll tell you the truth!"

"No we won't," said Pemphredo. "We can't rat on our sisters!"

"We don't have much choice, Phreddy," said

Deino. She raised her head from the huddle. "The Gorgons live in the Land of the Hyperborians," she said. "Now give us back our eye."

Perseus plucked the eyeball out of the helmet and tossed it in their direction. "Catch!"

"Where is it?" said Deino. "Did you catch it, Phreddy?"

"Not me," said Pemphredo. "Enyo?"

"I don't have it," said Enyo.

Perseus put on the Helmet of Darkness, but it began sparking again, and he didn't vanish. He was just banging his ankles together to activate his sandal wings when two flashes of light shimmered before him, revealing Athena and Hermes.

"Good work, Perseus!" said Athena. "Now let's go get Medusa."

"Who's there?" called Pemphredo. "Identify yourself!"

"Be careful!" called Deino. "Watch where you step!"

The Olympians ignored the Gray Sisters.

"I don't want you there," Perseus told the gods. "I can do it myself." He turned to face the north.

"Here I come, Medusa!" he cried. The helmet suddenly kicked into gear, and Perseus disappeared.

"What a foolish mortal," groaned Athena.

"Oh, let him have a whack at her," said Hermes. "If he fails, we can always step in."

"All right," agreed Athena. "But if Perseus doesn't behead Medusa, I'll definitely give her a big fat tail."

That said, they, too, vanished.

"Come on, Hades!" said Tisi. "We have to hurry!"

"We have to beat Perseus to the Land of the Hyperborians!" said Meg.

"We have to fly *now*!" said Alec.

Chapter XIII

BRIE CAREFUL!

"Don't drosis it, Furies," I said. "We'll astro-travel. We'll be in the Land of the Hyperborians in no time."

"You're forgetting, Hades," said Tisi. "Only gods can astro-travel. We're immortals, but we're not gods. And if you think you're going to leave us behind, you're sadly mistaken."

"Start warming up your engines," I told the Furies. "I'll be right back."

I dashed over to the Gray Sisters. They were crawling around pitifully, feeling for their eyeball. I picked it up and placed it in front of Enyo.

"I've got it!" she cried and she quickly popped it in. As I stood up to go, she turned and looked at me in surprise. On her, the eye was green.

An instant later, I was aboard the Air Furies shuttle, heading north.

"Admit it, Hades," Tisi called over her shoulder as we gained altitude. "I was right about waiting and listening to the Gray Sisters."

"Aren't you always?" I answered. Tisi's advice had been good, and I was a secure enough god to admit it. I wasn't too worried about Perseus beating us to the Land of the Hyperborians. It was a long way off, behind the back of the North Wind, which is about as far north as north gets. Perseus's puny little flapping sandals couldn't compete with the power of the Furies' great black wings.

"Do you Furies ever visit the Land of the Hyperborians?" I asked.

"No," said Tisi. "It's a land of happy beings who dance and feast all day."

"Hyperborians aren't mean to their mothers," said Meg.

"Ever!" said Alec.

It was a smooth flight except for a bit of turbulence above Mount Olympus. We soared over vast stretches of ice and snow. After a while, the snow gave way to green fields again. On we flew, and the green fields were replaced by sandy beaches. At last Tisi called, "Land of the Hyperborians ahead!"

We landed on a point of land lined with palm trees. A large sand dune rose behind the beach.

"This is what's at the back of the North Wind?" I said. "I was expecting mounds of snow."

"Don't ask me why," said Tisi. "But if you fly north long enough, you end up heading south."

The Furies sat down on the side of the dune to rest from their long flight. I passed around the ambrosia cheese crackers. Meg had wisely packed a few Necta-Colas.

"Remember telling me about the young mortal in Thebes?" I said as we ate. "The one who wouldn't help his mother bring in the goats from pasture?"

The Furies nodded.

"We gave him the Red Eye," said Meg.

"We made him think he was a goat," added Alec.

"Exactly," I said. "Could you give Perseus the Red

Eye and make him think he's already beheaded Medusa? And then fly him far, far away from the Gorgons?"

"Sure," said Tisi. "Why not?"

"I knew I could count on you Furies," I said.

A young Hyperborian mortal with tanned skin and sun-bleached hair came down the beach toward us. He carried a surfboard under one arm. Po had invented these wave-riding devices, and I was glad to see that they'd caught on.

"Hello!" I called to him. "I'm Hades, King of the Underworld."

"Awesome!" said the mortal. "I'm Troy of Hyperboria. Are you here to surf the point?"

"No, we're looking for some friends of ours," I told him.

"They have lovely snakes for hair," said Tisi.

"Oh, you mean the Gorg chicks?" Troy said. "Yeah, I know them. They live down the beach that way." He pointed. "Not far."

"Thanks, Troy," I said.

"Don't mention it, King," Troy said. "Catch you later!"

"Ready?" I asked the Furies.

"Not yet, Hades," said Meg. "It was a hard flight. We need more rest."

"I'll go scope things out," I told them. I borrowed Tisi's makeup mirror so I could look at Medusa, and started down the beach. I passed a few huts before I came to a high wall. There wasn't any gate. I pulled myself to the top of the wall and looked over. Cows, goats, and a magnificent white winged stallion were grazing in a field. At the far end of the field stood a large stone house. And beyond it lay what looked like a garden filled with statues. Stone statues.

I'd found Medusa.

I vaulted over the wall and made my way to the house. I rang the bell. When I heard someone coming, I turned around and looked into the mirror. The door opened. In the mirror I saw the reflection of a face with bulging eyes and big tusks, topped by a head full of squirming snakes.

"Riley?" I said. "Is that you?"

"Hades?" Riley gasped. "Come in, come in!" She turned away from the door. "Eno, Medusa, you won't believe this! We have company!"

I stepped into the Gorgons' house. Eno and

Medusa ran to greet me. Medusa wore a silky sea-blue bag over her head. Her snakes wriggled freely out of holes in the top.

"Oh, Hades!" Medusa said, overjoyed at seeing me. "How in the world did you find us?"

"Troy told me where you lived," I said.

"You met Troy?" Riley smiled, and I noticed that she and Eno had figured out some way to control the drool problem. "He's my favorite model."

"And the statues in your garden were a clue," I added.

"They were all accidents," said Medusa. "I've never purposely turned anyone to stone. Although I have a nice spot picked out for a statue of a certain goddess. No, I meant, how did you know we lived in the Land of the Hyperborians?"

"It's a long story," I said. "But the short answer is, the Gray Sisters."

"They squealed on us?" Medusa shook her head. "They wouldn't!"

"Don't be too hard on them," I told her. "Their eyeball was held hostage until they told where you were."

Eno held up a kamara. "I have to take a picture of you with my sisters, Hades," she said. "We don't get much company. Okay, make that no company. And I want to remember this moment. Smile, Riley! You, too, Hades! Say cheese, Medusa!"

"I'm smiling already," said Medusa from beneath her bag. "Just take the picture."

Click!

"Come out to my sculpture studio, Hades," Riley said. "I have so much to show you!"

"Another time," I said. "This isn't a social visit." And I quickly filled the Gorgons in on King Polydectes's plan. How he wanted to use Medusa's head for a weapon. How Perseus had sworn to bring him her head. And how Athena and Hermes were helping Perseus. By the time I finished my tale, Eno and Riley looked worried. I figured that under the bag, Medusa did, too.

But she surprised me by saying, "Athena is on her way here? Good. The timing is perfect."

"Perfect?" I said. "But Athena wants to give you a tail or help Perseus decapitate you!"

"I have something she'll want more than either

of those things," said Medusa. "I've learned a lot about Athena over the years. You may not know this, Hades, but Po arranged for me to join the Sea Nymph Intelligence Team."

Now I realized that the small white stitches near the top of her head bag spelled SNIT.

"Moon goddesses and sea nymphs are cousins," Medusa was saying. "So it wasn't much of a stretch. Over the years the other agents and I have kept a close eye on Athena. I know now why she cursed us, Hades. And I'm ready to meet her, head on. Good and ready!"

A loud knock sounded at the door.

I froze. What if Troy had given directions to Perseus? Or to Hermes and Athena?

"Another visitor?" said Eno. "I'll have to get more film!"

"Who's there?" called Riley.

There was no answer.

"Let's find out," said Medusa. She strode to the door and yanked it open.

On the stoop stood a trio of winged creatures with bulging eyes, boars' tusks, and snaky hair. I blinked. Had Athena Gorgonized other moon goddesses? What was going on?

"Hades!" said one of the creatures. "It's us, the Furies."

"We had our makeup kits," said Meg.

"We found some shells," said Alec, pulling what I'd thought was a tusk from under her lip. "We thought we'd have a little fun with Perseus before we give him the Red Eye."

"Great idea," said Medusa. I could tell she was smiling beneath her bag.

"Let's go to the point," said Riley. "Most everyone who flies in lands there."

Eno grabbed her kamara and we all set off down the beach. When we reached the point, the Gorgons and I hid ourselves behind the dune. The Furies lay down on the sand, pretending to sleep. Even if Perseus were invisible, the Furies would know when he landed. They could smell a mortal dekameters away.

While we waited, Medusa told me all about being a SNIT agent. She'd risen through the ranks quickly and had drawn some good assignments. But mainly she'd spied on Athena.

Without warning, the Furies rose suddenly into the air, screaming, flapping their wings, and rattling their scourges.

"Perseus has arrived," I whispered.

We peered over the top of the dune, watching the Furies fly around what looked like empty air. Then Tisi drew back her scourge and whipped it forward. Suddenly, Perseus appeared. Tisi had knocked my helmet off his head. It fell to the sand.

Perseus kept his eyes lowered as he tried to unclip the sickle from his girdle, all the while holding his big mirrored shield steady. But the shield was heavy, and it wobbled like crazy. Suddenly it barked out, "Surrender immediately! Surrender immediately!"

Perseus hit the ground. "All right!" he cried. "I surrender!"

The dope had forgotten about the shield's optional voice mechanism.

Alec snuck up behind him and snatched the shield away.

"Give that back!" Perseus cried. "No fair!"

"Hey, Perseus?" said Meg. "Look here! Quick!"

"Huh?" Perseus turned.

In front of him stood three hideously ugly winged monsters.

"I'm Medusa!" said Tisi.

"Nooo!" cried Perseus, squeezing his eyes shut.

"You've been stonified, Perseus," said Alec.

Perseus wiggled his fingers. He waved his arms. "But I didn't turn to stone!" he cried.

"It doesn't happen all at once," said Tisi. "Hardening into stone takes time."

"I see," said Perseus. "Does it hurt?"

"It's awful," said Alec.

"First your head feels heavy," said Tisi.

Perseus nodded slowly. "It does," he said.

"Then your feet feel like rocks," said Meg. "They get so heavy you can hardly walk."

Perseus took a few plodding steps. "Hardly walk," he murmured.

The Furies were giving Perseus a super Red Eye.

"Now is a good time for you to consider your pose," said Tisi.

"My pose?" Perseus sounded groggy.

"Yes," said Tisi. "The position you'll want to be in when you turn to stone for eternity."

"We recommend a heroic pose," said Meg.

"Something dramatic," said Alec.

"All right," said Perseus. "How's this?" He took a wide stance and put his hands on his hips. He stuck out his chin.

"Not bad," said Tisi. "How about showing your heroic spirit by raising one fist in the air?"

"Like so?" Perseus raised his right fist.

"Nice!" said Meg.

Behind the dune, the Gorgons and I were cracking up, but trying not to make any noise.

"What about raising a foot in the air?" Tisi said. "As if you were going to stomp on your enemies."

Perseus nodded, and lifted up his left foot.

"Now the chin a little higher!" said Alec.

"I'm laughing so hard I'm crying," Medusa whispered. "Turn your head, Hades. I have to take off this bag for a second to wipe my eyes."

My god-son threw his head back and thrust out his chin.

"Perfect!" said all three Furies together.

This heroic posture proved too much for Eno. She rose slowly from behind the dune and pointed her kamara at Perseus.

Click!

Startled, Perseus turned his head.

His eyes met those of the real Medusa.

ZAP! Perseus turned instantly to stone.

"Oops!" said Medusa.

Chapter XIV

STINKY!

I stared at the stone version of my god-son. "His mother is *not* going to be happy," I muttered.

The Furies gathered around the statue, hardly believing what had happened. The Gorgons joined them, and the six of them tsk-tsked and tusk-tusked over the stonification of Perseus.

I picked up my helmet. It was covered with sand, which, I suspected, could not be good for its inner workings.

Medusa came over to me. She had her bag on again. "I'm so sorry about Perseus."

"I know," I told her. "It wasn't your fault. I tried to stop him from coming to find you. I was afraid that something like this would happen." I shrugged. "What can you do?"

"We'll get our winged steed and fly him to our garden," Medusa offered. "We'll make a special place for him there. Maybe you can bring his mother to see him."

We turned to look at Perseus. His chin was thrust out, his fist was raised, and he had one foot up as if he was about to stomp on a roach. I doubted that Danaë would want to see him like this.

"We'll be back with the steed," said Medusa. She and her sisters flew off.

Tisi sighed. "It's hard to stop an arrogant young man from getting into trouble."

"I know," I said. "He's Zeus's son, but he's my god-son. His mother was counting on me to look after him, and I've failed."

A flash of light in the distance caught my eye.

"Astro-traveling gods heading in from the north," warned Meg.

I quickly clapped on the Helmet of Darkness.

Sand trickled into my eyes and mouth, but I vanished. And what a good thing! Three lights materialized, and there on the point stood Athena, Hermes, and Zeus.

Athena put her hand to her shoulder, checking to make sure that Hoo was in place.

Zeus yanked down his girdle, which had ridden up over his pot belly during the trip. He looked around and saw Tisi, Meg, and Alec.

"What are you Angries doing here?" Zeus asked.

"Furies," Tisi corrected him. "We're avenging."

"Go about it then. Scat!" said Zeus. "We Olympians have important business here."

"So do we," said Tisi. The Furies weren't afraid of any Olympian, not even the old T-bolt hurler himself. They sat down at the base of the dune. I sat down unseen beside them. I only hoped that my sandy helmet would hold its charge.

Zeus turned to Athena. "All right, daughter. Where is that son of mine?"

Athena was staring in horror at the statue on the beach. "It can't be him," she muttered.

Hermes flew in a circle around the statue

formerly known as Perseus. "It's him, all right," he said. "That sickle I gave him is solid rock. What a waste of a great tool!"

"That's him?" cried Zeus. "Why, I can't have any son of mine turned to stone! Who is responsible for this?"

"Hoo, hoo!" hooted Hoo.

"Medusa," said Athena quickly. "But let's not get into blame."

It wouldn't pay for Athena to play the blame game. After all, she was the one who had given Medusa her terrible statue-making power.

Zeus went over to Perseus. "What sort of pose is this?" he said. "He looks like an idiot." He tried to lower Perseus's arm. "Whoops!" he said, as the statue toppled over.

"Careful!" cried Athena. "Don't chip him!"

Hermes grabbed Perseus's arm and hauled him back to a standing position.

"Don't you know a chant that can change him back into a mortal?" said Zeus.

"I'm not sure," said Athena. "Most of the spells I've memorized are along the lines of horrible curses."

"Try something, daughter!" thundered Zeus. "Anything is better than this!"

"All right, all right," said Athena. "But I'm just winging it here, Dad. I've never done this before." She drew a breath and began to chant:

"Mortal Perseus, flesh and bone,
  Turned to statue made of stone,
  Stone will turn, when spell I offer,
  Into something paler and softer."

As we watched, Perseus's hard stony surface began to turn into something softer and paler. Athena's spell was working! But . . . Perseus didn't exactly look the way he used to.

Zeus went over to him now. He squinted his beady eyes and examined him all over. He sniffed. Then he poked Perseus's shoulder and licked his finger.

"Flying T-bolts, Athena!" Zeus cried. "You've turned my son into a giant stick of butter!"

"Butter?" Athena's eyes widened. "Well, that's a step in the right direction."

"Only until the sun gets hot," Hermes pointed out. "Then he'll melt."

"Fix him!" bellowed Zeus.

"I'll try," said Athena. "But back off, will you, Dad? The pressure is not helping." She leveled her gaze at the buttery Perseus and once more began to chant:

"Pale yellow Perseus, turned to butter,
Hear this spell that I now utter:
Butter turn bold, turn ready and rough!
Turn into stronger, firmer stuff."

As Athena spoke, buttery Perseus began to change again. His soft surface hardened. Blue veins appeared. He was clearly becoming bolder, rougher and firmer. And he started to give off a strong odor.

"Pee-yew!" said Zeus. "What is that stink?" He strode over to Perseus and poked him again. "Athena!" he thundered. "You've changed him into a great hunk of cheese!"

"Cheese?" said Athena, looking horrified. "Oh. Well. Um, what kind of cheese?"

"I don't know," said Zeus. He took another sniff. "It's really, really stinky. But this can be a good thing in a cheese. Anybody got any crackers?"

"No, Dad!" Athena cried. "I'm trying to get him back to his human form. He can't have big chunks taken out of him."

"One more spell, Athena," growled Zeus. "And this time, do it right. No fuzzy talk. Just say it straight out. Leave nothing to chance!"

Athena drew a breath and started chanting again:

"Butter to cheese and cheese to man,
Make that change now, if you can.
No tricks, no pranks, no jokes, no fuss,
Just turn back into Perseus."

And before our eyes, he did.

Perseus blinked. He looked around.

"Perseus!" exclaimed Athena. "Are you all right?"

"Of course," Perseus said. He unhooked the sickle from his belt and waved it in the air. "Medusa was here! Which way did she go?"

"Ha!" said Zeus. "That's my boy!"

Perseus turned to Zeus. "Dad?"

"Yes!" Zeus grinned. "I see you've inherited my bold spirit, my fearless heart. Good for you. Now go get Medusa. Don't let anything stop you, boy. And never, *ever* be afraid."

"I won't!" cried Perseus.

Just then wing beats sounded above us. We looked up and saw Riley and Eno riding on the back of the winged steed. It glided through the air, touched down on the sand, and galloped toward us. Eno and Riley had their eyes fastened on Athena. Riley was holding something behind her back.

"Slow down, you snake-heads!" cried Zeus. "You'll run us over!"

But the Gorgons didn't slow down. Their horse thundered toward us. Riley swept her arm forward, thrusting something into the faces of the Olympians. Suddenly the air filled with the screams of gods. And I saw what Riley was holding—

The severed head of Medusa!

Chapter XV

GORGON-ZOLA

Zeus and Hermes vanished instantly. So much for Zeus's advice to Perseus never, *ever* to be afraid.

Athena stood on the sand, as if turned to stone. The Furies averted their eyes from Eno and the awful head. Perseus fainted.

And me? I'd looked right at Medusa's face. I hoped I was standing in the way that would best represent me, K.H.R.O.T.U., for all eternity.

But I showed no sign of turning to stone.

My eyes found Riley. She sat on the back of the steed, smiling.

"Your sister!" I cried. "What have you done?"

Riley kept grinning. "Catch, Hades!" she shouted, and tossed me Medusa's head. The gory thing landed in my arms. I feared that I might drop to the ground in a faint like Perseus.

"The tusks are stone," said Riley. "The snakes are leather."

I looked closely. I was holding a Gorgon's head made of clay.

"I made several of them last spring, for the opening at my new gallery," Riley went on. "They sold out in the first ten minutes of the show."

"But why did you fly here with it?" I asked, tossing the head back to her. "To scare us?"

A shadow fell over the beach. I looked up and saw a flying Gorgon in a head bag. Medusa landed on the beach in front of Athena.

"To get rid of the two who fled," Medusa answered. "I knew Athena would remain."

"You'll be sorry," Athena snarled. "For now I shall finish what I started!" And she began to chant where she'd left off so many years ago:

"You've grown wings that are hard and shiny,
Now a tail with spikes shall sprout out of your—"

"You must look at me to curse me, Athena," Medusa said, cutting her off. She held the top of her head bag, as if ready to yank it off. "But if I take this off, you'll turn to stone."

Athena glared at Medusa. Beneath the bag, I was certain Medusa was glaring back.

At that moment Perseus sat up. He saw Medusa. He jumped to his feet. Flailing madly in the air with the Gorgon Scaler, he lunged for her.

But I lunged faster and tackled the boy. "Enough, Perseus!" I cried. I wrested the scaler from his hand and tossed it down the beach, out of his reach. Perseus kicked and fought, just as he had as an unruly little mortal boy. But I kept a godly grip on his wrists.

"Hear me, Athena," Medusa said. "I know now why you cursed my sisters and me."

"You were in my temple!" said Athena.

Medusa shook her head bag. "That was your excuse," she said. "But not your real reason. No, you hated us already. Admit it! You were jealous of our long, incredibly healthy, shiny hair. Take off your helmet, Athena."

Perseus stared at Medusa and stopped struggling.

I groaned. Medusa was her own worst enemy!

"I *never* remove my helmet!" cried Athena. "I was *born* wearing this helmet!"

"That's the problem," said Medusa. "It's given you a really bad case of helmet hair."

I couldn't believe where this was going. Did Medusa want that tail?

"I've made a study of you, Athena," Medusa went on. "I know how each night you sit before your dressing table mirror and remove your helmet. How you brush your thin, lifeless hair, trying to cover the bald patches on your scalp. How you rub oils and ointments and—"

"Stop!" cried Athena. "You've been spying on me!"

"Can you blame me?" Medusa asked. "I wanted to know all I could about the goddess who changed us into monsters. I thought if I found out why you did it, maybe I could find a way to convince you to change us back into our former shapes."

"Dream on!" Athena's face contorted into a vicious snarl. "I will destroy you!"

Medusa shrugged. "If you do, you'll never know how easy it is to get rid of helmet hair—forever."

"I don't need hair care advice from a Gorgon!" Athena shrieked.

Medusa held up a sea-blue bottle. "This is Moon Goddess Ultra-Super-Thickening Cream Rinse," she said. "When you're in and out of the salt water all day the way we used to be, it's murder on your hair. So my sisters and I experimented, and over the years, we concocted this cream rinse. It's got all sorts of exotic ingredients. We're the only ones who know the recipe. And believe me, it works."

Athena stared at the bottle.

I had a feeling it contained a pinch of Stygian riverwort.

"And you have to stop wearing your helmet XXIV/VII," Medusa went on. "That's what's given you the permanent ridge on the back of your head."

"Give me that bottle," snapped Athena. She reached out for it.

"Give it to you?" Medusa shook her head bag.

"No. But we could make a trade. You chant a de-gorgonizing spell, and I'll keep you supplied with Moon Goddess Cream Rinse forever."

Athena hesitated for a long moment. We all held our breath as her desire for vengeance fought with her desperation to get rid of her lifelong case of helmet hair. Finally, she said, "All right. I'll give it a try. Stand before me, Gorgons."

Medusa, Eno, and Riley lined up in front of Athena. The goddess of wisdom began to chant:

"Gorgons with claws and scales and wings,
Bug eyes, tusks, and snakes and things,
Change back, change back, and do it soon,
Once more become goddesses of the moon."

Before our eyes, Eno's and Riley's snakes drooped and became twists of hair. Their tusks vanished, their eyes receded, their scales turned to skin, their claws straightened into fingers, and their wings disappeared.

Tears of joy rolled down Eno's and Riley's cheeks.

Athena smiled. "Seems to have worked," she said.

I looked at Medusa. Her wings were gone and strands of hair cascaded out of the top of her head bag. But she hadn't taken off the bag.

"I need one more spell, Athena," she said.

"Ah, yes," said Athena. She raised her hands toward Medusa.

"Gorgon, with the power to lock
God or mortal into rock,
Now I free you from my curse,
With this spell-reversing verse."

"Are you brave enough to test the power of your words, Athena?" Medusa, gripped her head bag.

Athena hesitated for a moment, then nodded.

Slowly, Medusa drew the bag from her head.

Athena looked at her and smiled. "Worked—first try."

Now Medusa and her sisters cried and hugged each other, overjoyed not to be Gorgons any longer.

"Let's all go back to the house and celebrate," said Medusa at last. She eyed Athena. "You're invited, too," she said. "I don't believe in holding grudges."

Eno and Riley walked down the beach with Athena, the Furies, and Perseus. I caught a ride with Medusa on the beautiful white steed.

"This is Pegasus," said Medusa. "Someday I'll tell you where he came from. It's a long story. He is a beauty, isn't he?" She patted his milky white neck.

I had to agree. And the horse gave a much smoother ride than Air Furies.

We landed in the field beside the moon goddesses' house, dismounted, and went inside.

Tisi, Meg, and Alec excused themselves and went to take off their Gorgon makeup. When they came back, they looked like my Furies again.

"Keep an eye on Hoo for me, will you, Hades?" said Athena. "Riley said I could use her shower to wash my hair." Off she went.

The moon goddesses scurried off, too. They couldn't wait to wash their hair either, after not having any for so long.

"Hair," said Tisi. "It takes so much looking after."

"Snakes are care-free," said Meg.

"I never have a bad snake day, *ever!*" said Alec.

The Furies, Perseus, and I sat around a big coffee table, spread with papaya, pineapple, grapes, bread, and cheese. Perseus was very quiet. He hardly ate a thing. I could tell he was mulling over all that had happened.

Before long, the moon goddesses came in, looking the way I remembered them from that long-ago night at Athena's temple.

"Life is much better without a bag over my head!" exclaimed Medusa, pouring apple juice for Perseus, and some very primo nectar for the Furies and me.

Perseus jumped to his feet and faced Medusa. "I'm sorry I tried to decapitate you," he said. "You see, this evil king wants to marry my mother. I got him to agree that if I brought him your head so he could turn his enemies to stone, he'd marry this other princess and leave my mother alone." He sighed. "It was a really bad idea, but I was only trying to help my mother."

"Awwwwww," said all the Furies. Perseus had just become their favorite mortal.

I had a sudden thought. "Perseus," I said. "You could still give the king Medusa's head."

"I don't think so!" said Medusa.

"*That* Medusa's head," I said, pointing to Riley's sculpted head, which now hung on a hat rack by the front door.

Perseus went over and picked up the clay head. "This would fulfill my oath to bring Polydectes the head of Medusa," he said. "For this is indeed the head of Medusa."

"I modeled for it," said Medusa.

"And," I went on, "if Polydectes chooses to surround himself with his enemies and pull this head out of a bag . . ." I shrugged. "It won't be your fault if none of them turn to stone. It won't be your fault if they decide to attack Polydectes."

Perseus grinned. "Thank you, god-father. That is a perfect plan!"

"At the gallery, these Medusa heads go for thousands of drachmas," said Riley. "But you can have this one, Perseus, for free. I'll get you a bag to carry it in."

"Don't bother," said Perseus. "I have a magical wallet that—" He stopped, remembering exactly whose wallet it was.

"You may borrow the wallet," I told him. "But Persephone gets home on the first day of winter, so you'll have to return it by then."

"Thanks!" said Perseus. He opened the K.H.R.O.T.U. wallet, and Riley slid in the head.

Seeing my wallet made me think of Persephone. I had so much to tell her!

Now Athena appeared, patting her hair. It was the first time any of us had ever seen her without her helmet. "What do you think?" she asked, turning around.

She had thin brown hair. It didn't look at all like the flowing hair of the moon goddesses. But at least Athena had taken off her helmet. That was a start.

"Hoo, hoo!" cried Hoo, clearly impressed.

"Much improved," said Medusa encouragingly. "In a week, you won't believe the difference."

Athena smiled.

"More cheese, Hades?" said Medusa, holding out the platter to me.

I took a slice of bread and spread it with cheese. "Excellent cheese, by the way," I said. "It smells strong, almost like the cheesy Perseus."

"What?" said Perseus.

"Never mind," said Tisi. "Have some more apple juice."

"We keep cows, you know, Hades," Medusa said, taking some cheese, too. "This is a cheese we make ourselves. We call it Gorgon-zola."

I took a bite. "Mmmmm," I said. "I call it delicious."

Considering that Perseus had come to behead one of them, the moon goddesses were quite generous with him. Medusa even offered to lend him Pegasus to fly back to Seriphos.

"Yes!" said Perseus.

"He'll come straight home after," Medusa said. "He's quite a steed."

Athena turned to Riley. "That's a very frightening image." She pointed to a silvery metal Gorgon mask hanging on the wall. "Is that a piece of your sculpture?"

Riley nodded.

"I'd like to buy it from you," Athena said. "I want to fasten it to my breastplate to intimidate my enemies."

"I think we can make a deal." Riley smiled.

I stood up. "I have to get going," I said.

"Hold it," said Eno. "I want to take a group shot first. I have to immortalize this moment."

We all stood up, with the tallest of us—Athena, the Furies, and me, Hades—in back and the moon goddesses and Perseus in the front.

Eno looked through her viewfinder. "Squeeze closer together," she said. "That's it. Okay, smile, Perseus! You, too, Furies. Come on, let me see some fangs. Nice! Athena, the hair looks fabulous. Can't see Hoo. There he is. Okay, Hades. Think about Persephone. Good! Riley? Great. Come on! Say cheese, Medusa!"

Medusa smiled. "Gorgon-zola!"

Click!

Epilogue

That's the real story of Medusa. You can understand why Zeus didn't exactly want the world to know the truth—that he and Hermes freaked out and ran away from a sculpted head of Medusa.

It's also the real story of Perseus. But of course Zeus wanted to make his son look like a hero, so he spread it around that Perseus really did cut off the Gorgon's head. And his version ended up in most books of Greek myths.

When I finished writing *Say Cheese, Medusa!* I sent it to my good Titan buddy, Hyperion. He'd come to books late in life, after he retired from being a sun god. But once he discovered the joys of reading—especially *my* books—well, he just couldn't get enough of them.

Hyperion is a fast reader, but I wasn't expecting him to show up the next day. I'd gone over to di Minos Pizza Parlor for lunch, where I'd gotten one of the tables with a view of the Asphodel Fields. Cerberus was curled up at my feet, and I was enjoying a couple of slices while I skimmed *The Big Fat Book of Greek Myths*. I'd gone through a pile of napkins, because when you're eating pizza while reading a book, it's important to keep wiping the tomato sauce off your fingers. All of a sudden, Hyperion showed up, waving a copy of my manuscript. He wanted to talk about my story right away. But I made him sit down first and ordered him some lunch. Over lunch, we talked.

"Boy, howdy, Hades!" Hyperion said. "You've done it again. I had no idea that Medusa was really a moon goddess with long thick hair. What happened to her?"

"She and her sisters still live in the beach house in the Land of the Hyperborians," I said. "These days, mortals call it California."

"Now, what about Perseus?" asked Hyperion.

At the sound of Perseus's name, Cerberus began growling. That dog can hold a grudge forever.

"The sibyl told his grandpappy that Perseus would kill him one day," said Hyperion. "Did Perseus do that? Did he kill Acrisius?"

"Perseus decided to go back home to Argos," I said. "When King Acrisius heard he was coming, he fled to Larissa to hide. It so happened that Perseus stopped by Larissa on his way home to participate in some games. Perseus threw the discus. The wind blew it off course and the discus struck an old man in the crowd, killing him instantly. And guess who the old man turned out to be? Acrisius."

"Dawg!" said Hyperion. "That old guy did everything he could think of to keep the prophecy from coming true, but Perseus got him in the end. You can't fight fate, can you?"

"That's the truth," I said. "After his experience with the Gorgons, Perseus lost some of his boastfulness. He turned out to be a pretty good god-son after all. He managed to get rid of Polydectes. Then Dictys, the honest fisherman, became King of Seriphos and married Danaë. Perseus had lots more adventures. I wish I'd had room to put them all in the book."

"Me, too," said Hyperion. "So what's next, Hades? Whose story are you going to tell?"

"I'm thinking about Cupid," I told him. "Listen to this."

I started reading aloud from a chapter of *The Big Fat Book of Greek Myths*:

Aphrodite was jealous of the beautiful mortal Psyche. She ordered her son, the ultra-handsome god Cupid, to shoot Psyche with an arrow to make her fall in love with a horrible man. But when he saw Psyche, Cupid was so stunned by her beauty that he fell in love with her himself.

"I don't know, Hades." Hyperion shook his head. "Sounds a little mushy to me."

"That version does," I agreed. "But the real story isn't mushy at all. When he first saw Psyche, Cupid was having teen-god troubles. Greasy hair. Pimples. Braces. The works. He liked Psyche, but no way was he going to let her see him looking like a total dork. So he hatched a plan with his dad, Zeus, to kidnap Psyche. He thought he'd keep her a prisoner until he grew up and got better looking."

"What a sneaky trick!" said Hyperion.

"Really," I said. "What do you think of this title—*Nice Shot, Cupid!*"

"Works for me," said Hyperion. "These stories of yours just knock my socks off, old buddy, and I'll tell you what—I'd like to publish them."

"What do you mean?" I asked him.

"You know," Hyperion said. "I'll have a famous artist draw some really fine pictures for the covers. Maybe draw some maps. Then I'll get the stories printed up and turned into books. I'll put my name on it, too, just to let everybody know I'm one hundred percent behind every word. Now, how can you turn down an offer like that?"

"Sounds good to me, Hyperion," I said.

We shook on it then, and to my surprise, the old Titan even picked up the check for lunch.

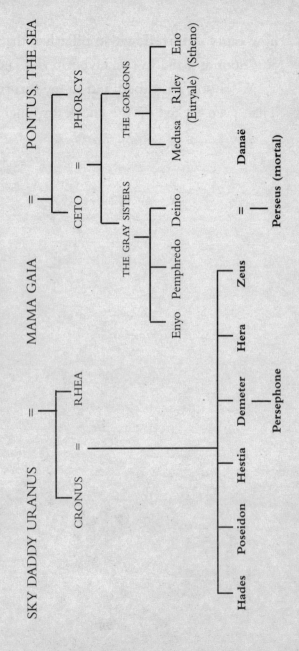

King Hades's
QUICK-AND-EASY
Guide to the Myths

Let's face it, mortals, when you read the Greek myths, you sometimes run into long, unpronounceable names—like *Polydectes* and *Aganippe*—names so long that just looking at them can give you a great big headache. Not only that, but sometimes you mortals call us by our Greek names, and other times by our Roman names. It can get pretty confusing. But never fear! I'm here to set you straight with my quick-and-easy guide to who's who and what's what in the myths.

Acrisius [uh-KRIZ-ee-us]: evil King of Argos, who was told by a seer that his grandson would kill him; husband of Aganippe, father of Danaë, grandfather of Perseus.

Aganippe [ag-uh-NIP-ee]: Queen of Argos, wife of Acrisius, mother of Danaë, grandmother of Perseus.

Alec: see **Furies**.

ambrosia [am-BRO-zha]: food that we gods must eat to stay young and good-looking for eternity.

Aphrodite [af-ruh-DIE-tee]: goddess of love and beauty. The Romans call her **Venus**.

Apollo [uh-POL-oh]: god of light, music, and poetry; Artemis's twin brother. The Romans couldn't come up with anything better, so they call him **Apollo**, too.

Ares [AIR-eez]: god of war. The Romans call him **Mars**.

Artemis [AR-tuh-miss]: goddess of the hunt and the moon, Apollo's twin sister. The Romans call her **Diana**.

Asphodel Fields [AS-fuh-del]: the large region of the Underworld where nothing grows except for a weedy gray-green plant; home to the ghosts of those who were not-so-good-but-not-so-bad in life.

Athena [uh-THEE-nuh]: goddess of wisdom, as well as weaving, and war. Wears a Gorgon mask on the breastplate of her armor. The Romans call her **Minerva**.

Athens [ATH-enz]: major city in Greece, sacred to Athena.

Cerberus [SIR-buh-russ]: my fine, III-headed pooch, guard dog of the Underworld.

Ceto [SEE-toe]: part woman, mostly sea snake, Ceto is wife (and sister—don't ask) of Phorcys and mother of the Gorgons and the Gray Sisters.

Charon [CARE-un]: river-taxi driver; ferries the living and the dead across the River Styx.

Cronus [CROW-nus]: my dad, a truly sneaky Titan, who once ruled the universe. The Romans called him **Saturn**.

Cyclops [SIGH-klops]: any of three one-eyed giants, Lightninger, Shiner, and Thunderer, children of Gaia and Uranus, and uncles of us gods. More than one are **Cyclopes** [sigh-KLO-peas].

Danaë [DAN-uh-ee]: Princess of Argos, daughter of Acrisius and Aganippe, mother of Perseus.

Delphi [DELL-fie]: an oracle in Greece on the southern slope of Mount Parnassus, where a sibyl is said to predict the future.

Demeter [duh-MEE-ter]: my sister, goddess of

agriculture and total gardening nut. The Romans call her **Ceres**.

Dictys [DICK-tis]: an honest fisherman; brother to evil King Polydectes of Seriphos.

Dionysus [die-uh-NIE-sus]: god of wine and good-time party guy. The Romans call him **Bacchus**.

Dodona [dough-DOUGH-nuh]: a land where talking oak trees reveal the will of Zeus.

drosis [DRO-sis]: short for **theoexidrosis** [thee-oh-ex-uh-DRO-sis], old Greek-speak for "violent god sweat."

Elysium [eye-LIZH-ee-um]: Underworld region of eternal daylight and endless apple orchards where ghosts of heroes and of those who were good in life party on.

Eno: see **Gorgon**.

Furies [FYOOR-eez]: three winged immortals with red eyes and serpents for hair who pursue and punish wrongdoers, especially children who insult their mothers; their full names are Tisiphone [tih-ZIH-fuh-nee], Megaera [MEH-guh-ra], and Alecto, but around my palace, they're known as Tisi, Meg, and Alec.

Gaia [GUY-uh]: Mother Earth, married to Uranus, Father Sky (Sky Daddy); mom to the Titans, Cyclopes, Hundred-Handed Ones, Typhon, and other giant monsters, and granny to us Olympian gods. The Romans call her **Tellus.**

Gorgon [GOR-gun]: any of the three moon-goddess sisters whom Athena turned into winged snake-haired monsters. Their full names are Euryale [you-RY-uh-lee] (nick-named Riley), Sthenno [STHEE-no] (Eno for short), and Medusa.

Gorgonize [GOR-gun-ize]: to turn to stone, or petrify, as with fear.

Gray Sisters: also known as **Graiai** [GREYE-eye]; the swanlike older sisters of the Gorgons, who live on Mount Atlas. They were born with gray skin and gray hair. They must share a single eyeball and just one tooth. Their names are Enyo, Pemphredo [pem-FRAY-doh], and Deino [DAY-noh].

Hades [HEY-deez]: K.H.R.O.T.U., King Hades,

Ruler of the Underworld, that's me. I'm also god of wealth, owner of all the gold, silver, and precious jewels in the earth. The Romans call me **Pluto**.

Hephaestus [huh-FESS-tus]: lame god of the forge, metalworkers, jewelers, and blacksmiths. The Romans call him **Vulcan**.

Hera [HERE-uh]: my sister, Queen of the Olympians, goddess of marriage. The Romans call her **Juno**. I call her the Boss.

Hermes [HER-meez]: god of shepherds, travelers, inventors, merchants, business executives, gamblers, and thieves; messenger of the gods; escorts the ghosts of dead mortals down to the Underworld. The Romans call him **Mercury**.

Hestia [HESS-tea-uh]: my sister; goddess of the hearth; a real homebody. The Romans call her **Vesta**.

Hyperborians [hi-per-BOR-ee-uns]: inhabitants of the Land of Hyperborians in the far, far north; a happy, laid-back people.

Hyperion [hi-PEER-ee-un]: a way-cool Titan, once in charge of the sun and all the light in the universe. Now retired, he owns a cattle ranch in the Underworld. Has a taste for good books.

Hypnos [HIP-nos]: god of sleep; brother of Thanatos (the god of death); son of Nyx, or night. Shhh! he's napping.

ichor [EYE-ker]: god blood.

immortal: a being, such as a god or possibly a monster, who will never die—like me.

Medusa [meh-DOO-suh]: the Gorgon who Athena cursed with the power to turn whoever looked at her to stone.

Meg: see **Furies**.

mortal: a being who one day must die; I hate to be the one to break this to you, but *you* are a mortal.

Mount Olympus [oh–LIM-pes]: the highest mountain in Greece; its peak is home to all the major gods, except for my brother, Po, and me.

nectar [NECK-ter]: what we gods like to drink; has properties that invigorate us and make us look good and feel godly.

oracle [OR-uh-kul]: a sacred place where a seer or sibyl foretells the future, sometimes used to refer to the sibyl herself, or her prophecy.

Pegasus [PEG-uh-sus]: Medusa's white-winged steed.

Persephone [per-SEF-uh-nee]: goddess of spring and my Queen of the Underworld. The Romans call her **Proserpina**.

Perseus [PER-see-us]: son of Danaë and Zeus, reputed (falsely) to have slain the Gorgon Medusa by looking at her in a shield and beheading her.

Phorcys [FOR-kiss]: wise old man of the sea, has a fish tail. Husband to Ceto and father of the Gorgons and the Gray Sisters.

Polydectes [poll-ee-DECK-teez]: evil king of Seriphos who wants to get rid of Perseus and marry Danaë; brother of Dictys.

Poseidon [po-SIGH-den]: my bro Po; god of the seas, rivers, lakes, and earthquakes; claims to have invented horses as well as the surfboard and the doggie paddle. The Romans call him **Neptune**.

Riley: see **Gorgon**.

Roman numerals: what the ancients used instead
of counting on their fingers. Makes you glad
you live in the age of Arabic numerals and
calculators, doesn't it?

I	1	XI	11	XXX	30
II	2	XII	12	XL	40
III	3	XIII	13	L	50
IV	4	XIV	14	LX	60
V	5	XV	15	LXX	70
VI	6	XVI	16	LXXX	80
VII	7	XVII	17	XC	90
VIII	8	XVIII	18	C	100
IX	9	XIX	19	D	500
X	10	XX	20	M	1000

Seriphos [SEHR-uh-fos]: island where the wooden
box with Danaë and Perseus inside washed
ashore; kingdom of Polydectes.

sibyl [SIB-ul]: a mortal woman said to be able to
foretell the future; a prophetess.

Stygian Naiads [STY-jee-un NIGH-ads]: also
known as **Naiads of the Styx**, a special
breed of naiad, or water nymph, the Stygian

Naiads have sprightly women's bodies but, because of a curse, they have dogs' heads, of which they are deeply ashamed.

Tartarus [TAR-tar-us]: the deepest pit in the Underworld and home of the Punishment Fields where burning flames and red hot lava eternally torment the ghosts of the wicked.

Thanatos [THAN-uh-toss]: god of death; brother of Hypnos.

Tisi: see **Furies**.

Underworld: my very own kingdom, where the ghosts of dead mortals come to spend eternity.

Zeus [ZOOS]: rhymes with *goose*, which pretty much says it all; my little brother, a major myth-o-maniac and cheater, who managed to set himself up as Ruler of the Universe. The Romans call him **Jupiter**.

Kate McMullan is the author of more than fifty books for children, including several collaborations with her husband, noted illustrator, Jim McMullan. Their latest, *I Stink!,* stars a garbage truck with attitude.

Kate and her husband live in New York City and Sag Harbor with their daughter and their two mewses, George and Wendy.

Visit Kate at www.katemcmullan.com